Gone was the work-at-home mom he was used to

In her place was a blond bombshell—slender but with curves in all the right places. And legs that seemed to go on for miles.

"Is that a new dress?" Reece asked, his voice much hoarser than usual. But he couldn't do anything about that—the second he'd laid eyes on Sarah, most of the blood had left his head and pooled about three feet south.

Her cheeks heated and she glanced down, her hand playing uncomfortably in the silky skirt. "It is. I found it at the mall last week, when I was picking up shoes for Rose."

"You look good."

"Really?" Her smile was tentative.

"Yeah." Oh, yeah. Good enough to have his libido leaping to life after nearly a year of complete and total dormancy. And his body was now reminding him—in very uncomfortable detail—just how long it had been since he'd held a woman in his arms.

Dear Reader,

I think the best fiction is a blend of reality and make-believe. In *From Friend to Father*, I've done just that. While I've never been a surrogate mother, I have lost a very dear friend. And while I don't have twin boys, I do have three young sons—and the trouble Justin and Johnny get into in this novel stems directly from things my own sons have done through the years.

From flushing my cell phone, and various other objects, down the toilet to literally swinging from the chandelier above my dining-room table, my boys have tried just about everything there is to try—not to mention inventing a few new things along the way. They've broken bones, fallen down stairs, jumped into pools without knowing how to swim and generally caused mischief and mayhem in every place imaginable. My youngest even spent two weeks in the NICU as an infant, and the prayers Sarah utters as she sits with baby Rose echo my own prayers as I watched my child struggle for life.

But like Sarah, I wouldn't trade one moment of the time I've had with my children. Parenting is a journey—one filled with moments of incredible exhilaration and others filled with frightening despair. In *From Friend to Father*, I've tried to communicate the good times as well as the bad, and I hope I've succeeded.

Thank you so much for letting me—and my stories—into your lives and hearts. I love to hear from readers via my Web site, www.tracywolff.com, or on my blog, www.sizzlingpens.blogspot.com. I hope you enjoy *From Friend to Father*—I look forward to hearing from you.

All my best,

Tracy Wolff

FROM FRIEND TO FATHER
Tracy Wolff

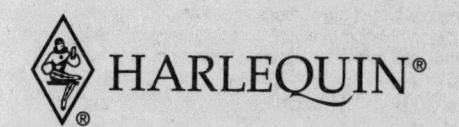

HARLEQUIN®

TORONTO • NEW YORK • LONDON
AMSTERDAM • PARIS • SYDNEY • HAMBURG
STOCKHOLM • ATHENS • TOKYO • MILAN • MADRID
PRAGUE • WARSAW • BUDAPEST • AUCKLAND

ISBN-13: 978-0-373-71568-8

FROM FRIEND TO FATHER

www.eHarlequin.com

Printed in U.S.A.

ABOUT THE AUTHOR

Tracy Wolff collects books, English degrees and lipsticks and has been known to forget where—and sometimes who—she is when immersed in a great novel. At six she wrote her first short story—something with a rainbow and a prince—and at seven she forayed into the wonderful world of girls' lit with her first Judy Blume novel. By ten she'd read everything in the young adult and classics sections of her local bookstore, so in desperation her mom started her on romance novels. And from the first page of the first book, Tracy knew she'd found her lifelong love. Now an English professor at her local community college, she writes romances when she's not chasing after her three young sons.

Books by Tracy Wolff

HARLEQUIN SUPERROMANCE

For Mom and Connie—
two of the greatest women I know

Acknowledgments

To Wanda, whose help and support
has made me a better writer.

And, as always, to Emily.
Thanks for all that you do.

PROLOGUE

SHOCK AND GRIEF mixed with the anger and disbelief that had taken root inside of her four days before until it was all Sarah Martin could do to sit still for the drawn-out service.

Vanessa was dead.

Her best friend was dead.

Killed last week in a car crash that was nobody's fault.

Somehow the fact that it really had been just an accident made acceptance that much harder. How could the death of a beautiful thirty-three-year-old woman be no one's fault? The other driver had simply lost control of his SUV on the rain-slicked road, despite going a reasonable thirty miles an hour in the fifty-mile-an-hour zone.

He'd spun out, crossed the center line and collided with the Prius Vanessa had bought six months before to do her part to help the environment. The little car hadn't stood a chance against the gas-guzzling behemoth that slammed into it. And that quickly, Van was gone.

But how could she be gone, Sarah wondered almost wildly. Why now, when things were finally going so right for her? How could Vanessa be *gone* when they'd had plans to shop for maternity clothes together?

The baby kicked inside of her—a swift one-two shot to the bladder that had Sarah crossing her legs and praying for the funeral to end. Running a hand over the belly that had recently outgrown her regular clothes, Sarah rubbed it soothingly. The baby responded by kicking again—harder—and she pondered, fleetingly, if she was carrying the next Evander Holyfield. Lord knows, the kid certainly hit like a world champ and his or her birth was still four months away.

At the front of the church, the priest murmured the last few words of his eulogy. Thank God. She couldn't take much more of this without screaming her fear and confusion at the world.

Yet when it was over, when it was finally time to exit the narrow, wooden pews, Sarah found she had a hard time moving. She'd wanted to leave from the second she'd arrived at the church, had wanted to be as far away from the pretty lavender casket in front of the altar as she could get.

But now, all she could think was that this was the absolute last time she and Vanessa would ever share a space. There would be no more cups of coffee at the local coffeehouse, no more quick trips to the mall. No more pizza-and-movie nights with the boys when Reece was out of town. Nothing but months and years of empty afternoons stretched before her.

But she couldn't stay here forever. The pallbearers were taking Vanessa's casket away, preparing to load it into the hearse for the final trip to the cemetery. Sarah should go—was expected to go. But she didn't think she could take any more goodbyes without cracking.

Sarah walked slowly down the aisle of the church, pain heavy within her. When she got outside, she caught her first glimpse of Reece since that awful day at the hospital. He looked terrible—tired, worn-out and with the same bruised, shell-shocked look she'd seen this morning when she'd glanced in the mirror.

As she looked at him, she realized there was an air of rage about him that she lacked, a fury that went somehow deeper than her own pain and horror.

When that car had lost control in the rain, Sarah had lost her best friend. But Reece—Reece had lost his wife, his best friend and his soul mate, all wrapped up into one vivacious, wonderful package. Was there any doubt, then, why he looked like he wanted to take on what was left of his world?

"Reece." She stopped in front of him, laid a hand on his arm. "I'm so sorry."

His confused brown eyes met hers, searching as if he was trying to figure out who she was. "Sarah." The word sounded forced, almost strangled.

"Call me, if you need anything at all."

His gaze dropped to her stomach, to the bump that was beginning to show. "The baby—" His voice broke and she reached out to cover his hand with her own.

"Don't worry about that now. We've got plenty of time to figure it all out. The baby's not due for months yet."

He nodded jerkily, as if he heard the words she was

saying, but couldn't quite understand them. She couldn't blame him—getting through the day was hard enough without facing her suddenly uncertain future.

She wrapped her arms around him and hugged him tightly. "We'll get through this, Reece." She felt the need to say the words to him, even though she wasn't sure she believed them herself.

He patted her back almost absently, then turned away when someone called his name. She tried not to feel bereft, tried not to blame him for his lack of response. It wasn't his fault that he and Vanessa were the last two people she had on earth to rely on. No more than it was his fault that Vanessa's death had completely shattered her.

It had shattered him, as well.

Blinking back tears, Sarah headed to her car. She was nothing to him, she reminded herself. Just his dead wife's best friend.

And the mother of his unborn child.

CHAPTER ONE

SHE DIDN'T KNOW whether to laugh or cry. So Sarah did what she always did when she had the choice—threw back her head and laughed herself silly. Then dived for the shut-off valve at the base of the toilet that was currently overflowing onto the crimson tile floor she had laid herself a year ago.

Once the water flow was cut off—and the floor mopped up—she turned to Johnny, the oldest of her five-year-old twins. "Does someone want to explain to me what happened *this* time?"

"Pirate Jack was a bad, bad pirate, Mommy," Johnny said in his earnest little boy voice, his blue eyes wide with sincerity. "He had to walk the plank."

"Yeah," Justin said. "He's a criminal, Mommy. He deserves a terrible pun-pun-pu—"

"Punishment." Johnny rolled his eyes with all the annoyance of a big brother—as if far more than five minutes separated the two of them.

"Walked the plank?" Sarah shook her head in amazement. "Into the toilet? Again? I thought we talked about this." Over and over and over again, they had talked until she felt like a broken record. Or worse, a useless one.

"That's where Jasper went when he died, Mommy. Remember? We gave him a hero's funeral."

Of course she remembered. Her brother—her wonderful, irresponsible, fun-loving brother—had been babysitting the twins when the fish had died and, for whatever reason, had decided to give the goldfish a "proper" funeral. Complete with a burial at sea, accomplished by flushing him down the guest bathroom toilet.

Too bad Tad hadn't thought to warn the twins that not everything that went into the toilet actually made it down the pipes and out to sea. It might have saved her budget—not to mention what little sanity she had left.

For the past three months, she—and her trusty plumber—had rescued everything from superheroes and toy soldiers to the baby's rattle and hair bows from the toilet and the pipes below it. But Pirate Jack, he was a new one. It was definitely his first trip down the flusher.

Turning back to the toilet, she tried to locate some part of the toy still sticking into the bowl—an arm, a leg, a head, she wasn't picky. But alas, Jack had made it all the way into the pipes before getting stuck.

"Which Pirate Jack was it?" she asked, feeling the need to clarify as the boys had about twenty variations on the pirate theme. Please don't let it be the big one her brother—

"The one Uncle Tad got us."

Of course it had to be that one. That one was larger than her fist and had hard plastic arms and legs shooting off in all directions. She was shocked the thing had actually made it out of the bowl.

With a sigh, Sarah headed downstairs to get the plunger out of the garage. Not that she had a hope of getting the stupid toy out—as big as it was, she was almost positive it was well and truly lodged in the pipe. Which meant calling Vince the plumber. She sighed. Which meant at least two hundred dollars she couldn't afford to spend this month, not with the two visits Vince had already paid to their house on top of the unexpected car repairs she'd had to deal with last week. The new transmission had eaten up most of her discretionary income for the month. She really hated to dip into her savings, but it wasn't like she had a choice. Unless, by some miracle, the plunger actually worked.

After wrestling with the plunger for fifteen minutes, Sarah gave up. It was time to call Vince. She reached for the phone—what did it say about her life that he was number two on her speed dial?

"Boys," she said softly as she checked on them. They were playing in their room, building blocks into huge towers then knocking them down with their trucks. "I'm going to be on the phone for a few minutes. Keep it down, okay? The baby's sleeping."

"Okay, Mommy," Justin said sweetly, even as his brother rolled his eyes.

"She's always asleep," complained Johnny.

"That's what two-month-old babies do, sweetie. They sleep a—" She cut off in midsentence as Angie, Vince's full-time receptionist, answered the phone. And how sick was it that she knew the other woman's name?

"Hi, Angie. It's Sarah Martin. My toilet's clogged again."

"What'd the boys flush this time?" Angie asked, laughter evident in her voice.

"Their favorite pirate toy had to walk the plank." Despite the drain on her finances, she had a hard time keeping the amusement out of her voice, as well. Really, who on earth—besides five-year-old boys—would ever think to do such a thing?

"Nice one. Give me a second and I'll see if Vince can get over there this morning."

"No problem. I'll be home all—"

The smoke alarm in the kitchen went off. "Oh, no! The cookies!"

Sarah ran down the stairs, her first thought to stop the screeching before it woke the baby. But as soon as she hit the first floor, she realized that was easier said than done. The entire downstairs was thick with smoke as she'd left the cookies in—she glanced at the clock— nearly twenty minutes longer than she should have.

Opening the back door and various windows on her way to the kitchen, she waved frantically at the smoke detector in the hallway, trying to clear the smoke from beneath it.

"The cookies are burnded?" asked Justin, lower lip quivering, as she rushed into the kitchen and pulled the blackened treats from the oven.

"Burnded doesn't quite cover it," she muttered to herself. They were so blackened she feared they'd burst into flames any second. With a sigh she dumped them—

tray and all—into the sink and ran water over them. It was the second batch she'd massacred that week.

"Not again," wailed Johnny over the scream of the smoke detector. "Mommy, you promised we'd have cookies today."

"And we will. I—"

"Sarah?" Angie came back on the line.

"Shh." She turned a stern look on her boys, who ignored it and continued to whine about the lack of chocolate-chip cookies in their lives. "Yes, Angie?" she said, straining to hear the receptionist.

"Vince can be there around two o'clock. Is that okay?"

"Sure. Why not?"

"It sounds like you've got your hands full there."

"What?"

"It sounds like—never mind." Angie laughed. "I'll talk to you later, Sarah."

"What?"

The phone went dead in her hand as Sarah realized that not all of the noise lambasting her ears was from the boys and the smoke alarm. Some of the screams were coming from her baby girl who was now wide-awake, despite the fact that she should have slept for at least another hour.

"Coming, Rose," she called as she headed up the stairs, the boys trailing behind her. Their tears had turned to shouts of delight the second they heard their sister's cries. The rule was that as soon as Rose woke up from her nap, quiet time was over. Silence was definitely not their natural state.

Sarah burst into her daughter's room, and scooped Rose from the crib, holding the small, trembling body to her chest. "It's okay, baby. Nothing to be scared of. Mama's here."

The baby continued to wail despite Sarah's presence, her cries getting louder with each high-pitched scream from the smoke detector. Would the stupid alarm *never* go off? To protect Rose's delicate hearing, Sarah covered the ear not pressed to her chest with her hand.

Murmuring to the baby, she went downstairs. She wasn't sure if Rose was hungry yet, but the comfort of a pacifier would do a lot to calm her.

Sarah barely cleared the bottom step when the doorbell rang. Vince must have been able to get away earlier than expected. Before she reached the door the boys rushed past her, their voices raised in war whoops of celebration. They loved watching Vince work, and she was beginning to suspect that they were breaking the toilet on purpose—a sneaky ploy to see the plumber again and again. Sarah had just enough time to register that Justin's face was streaked with red lines while Johnny's was covered with black ones, before they swung open the door.

Her boys paused in mid-war whoop. Vince wasn't standing on the other side of the threshold.

Reece Sandler was.

She'd never seen her best friend's husband look more uncomfortable, despite his carelessly styled brown hair and the designer clothes that showed off his six-foot-four-inch frame to its best advantage.

On the bright side, the sudden influx of hot September air must have been just what the smoke detector needed as it finally stopped shrieking.

Blessed silence filled the room and Sarah took a moment to compose herself. But a moment wasn't long enough to combat the six and a half months' worth of fury seething inside her.

A better woman might have bitten her tongue before making a comment. A good woman would certainly have made things easier on the man. But Sarah had never claimed to be trying for sainthood, and she had a lifetime of anger and hurt stored up inside of her.

Aw, SHIT, was all Reece could think as his gaze collided with the baby he'd spent the past few months pretending didn't exist. First, he'd abandoned Sarah for the last half of her pregnancy. Then he hadn't made it to the hospital when the baby was born. And now, over two months had passed and, despite Sarah's insistent phone calls, he'd yet to visit it.

Her, he reminded himself. Not *it.* The baby was a girl.

His baby was a girl.

Shame ate at him, warring with the anger and guilt and sorrow that had taken up residence in his soul two hundred and nine days ago. This baby was his responsibility—his alone—yet he'd abandoned Sarah to deal with Rose. The fact that he hadn't wanted her to begin with—and still didn't have a clue what to do with her—was no excuse.

"To what do we owe this honor?" Sarah's hostile tone—so at odds with her normally sunny disposition—

wasn't totally unexpected. Yet it still hurt in a way he was completely unprepared for. This was Van's best friend and what she thought of him mattered. That she had every right to think of him as a total rat didn't make her disgust any easier to bear.

"Well, are you going to answer me?"

"You haven't—" His voice gave out and Reece had to clear his throat several times before he was able to continue. "You haven't cashed the checks I sent."

"That's why you're here? Because of the *money?*"

He pulled his gaze away from the pink-and-purple-clad baby in her arms and met Sarah's. Her blue eyes were filled with rage, brimming with the stuff until he couldn't help thinking it was a miracle he hadn't been struck dead on her doorstep.

"Look, can I come in?" he asked, discomfort giving way to annoyance. He knew he had a lot to apologize for and he was man enough to do it. But he'd be damned if he'd do it in front of the entire neighborhood.

Those indigo eyes darkened even as they narrowed, and he was sure she would slam the door in his face. But finally, when he was really starting to sweat, she shrugged and opened the door wider. Then turned and walked away without so much as a backward glance.

"Uncle Reece, Uncle Reece!" Justin grabbed his hand and yanked—at least he thought it was Justin. It had been a long time since he'd seen the twins and with all that paint on their faces, it was difficult to tell them apart. "We missed you."

Guilt hit him again, hard. Before Van's death, he'd

spent a lot of time with the boys. Their father—Sarah's husband—had walked out when they were babies and Reece had been the closest thing to a father figure they had. When Van had died, he hadn't just cut himself off from Sarah and his baby, but also from the boys he'd considered his nephews.

"I missed you guys, too." He ran a hand over each little blond head.

"Did you bring us something?" Johnny asked. There was a time when he and Van would never have considered dropping by without some small present for the boys—a couple Matchbox cars, packs of gum, new balls. Yet another tradition that had died with his wife.

"I'm sorry, guys. I forgot. But I promise I'll bring something with me the next time."

"Don't make promises you can't keep." Sarah was back, probably wondering what was taking him so long.

"I plan on keeping that promise." He found himself reluctant to leave the boys—they were a bit of normalcy in a world turned violently upside down.

Her snort was not encouraging.

"Look, Sarah—"

"Boys, go on upstairs and wash the makeup off your faces."

"But, Mom, we're Indians."

"Still?" She raised an inquiring eyebrow.

"Yeah!"

"Then you'd better go be Indians before Rose needs another nap."

"Aww, Mom! Already?"

"Not yet, but soon. Her nap was cut short, remember."

"Yes." Johnny sighed, hanging his head dejectedly. He looked for all the world like a kid who'd just found out that Santa Claus didn't exist. Then Justin came up behind him and hit him on the head with a makeshift tomahawk. That's all it took to send the two of them running up the stairs, laughing and hollering for all they were worth.

Reece watched them go. Otherwise he would have to look at Sarah. Or worse, the baby.

As he avoided her gaze, he realized the house was trashed. Toys were scattered everywhere, along with sippy cups and baby paraphernalia. Stacks of clean clothes sat at the bottom of the stairs while a pile of clean diapers and a box of wipes graced Sarah's normally immaculate dining-room table.

He cleared his throat, searched for something to say. "Is it always like this around here?"

"Like what?"

"So…crazy?" As soon as the word was out, he knew he'd made a vital mistake.

"I'm a single mom with twin boys, a home business and a baby I had no intention of having to care for after her birth." Sarah's voice turned virulent. "So, yeah, it's pretty much always like this."

The bitterness made him feel even lower—something he hadn't thought was possible. Taking a deep, bracing breath he turned to really look at Sarah. And tried to ignore the wholly inappropriate jolt he felt when her gaze met his.

It was the same jolt he'd felt every time she'd looked at him for the past eight years. The same one he'd tried desperately to ignore—to pretend didn't exist. And his tactics didn't work any better today than they had in years past.

Was it any wonder he'd run so far and fast when Vanessa died? Because he was a perverted bastard who, even while grieving for his wife, couldn't get over his strange fascination with her best friend.

But as he looked at Sarah—really saw her—he realized that the woman he knew was nowhere to be found. The competent, in-control, perfectly groomed Sarah was gone. In her place was a woman he barely recognized. A woman who was sad, vulnerable, beaten down. A woman whose utter defenselessness somehow made her seem even more attractive.

She looked like hell—worse than he'd ever seen her, except right after Mike had taken off. She'd lost weight she couldn't afford to lose, so much that a gentle breeze could blow her over. Her eyes were ringed with such dark circles it seemed like someone had punched her. Her skin was sallow and her hair hung in short, limp strands around her face.

He'd done this to her—with his selfishness and in-ability to deal with his issues. *He'd* turned her from the beautiful, self-confident woman he'd first met shortly after he'd started dating Vanessa into this washed-out—wrung-out—version of herself.

And, sick ass that he was, he was as attracted—maybe even more attracted—to this woman than he'd been to the savvy, perfectly coiffed businesswoman.

Burying his traitorous feelings as deeply as he could,

he searched for a way to restart the conversation, to ease into the subject he'd been dreading for far too long. No easy way to do this, no way to absolve him of the mistakes he'd made.

"I'm sorry, Sarah." The words burst from him. "I'm so very sorry."

"For what?"

At first he thought she was asking what he had to be sorry for. Then he realized she wanted to know *which* of his many transgressions he was apologizing for.

"For everything. I let you down."

Her lips twisted in a smirk that wasn't even remotely amused. "I guess you could say that."

The baby moved, her little arms flailing as she wailed. "What's wrong with her?"

"She's tired and hungry. She fell asleep without her bottle earlier."

"Bottle? You're not breast-feeding her?"

Sarah stiffened at the unintentional censure in his voice and Reece could have kicked himself.

"I started her on bottles right after she was born because I *assumed* that she would be going home from the hospital with her *father.* By the time I figured out that you really weren't coming for her, it was too late. My milk never came in properly."

She crossed the room, pulled a ready-made bottle out of the fridge and popped it into the microwave.

"I thought microwaves—" He refused to say one more word that could be taken as criticism by Sarah. He was in the wrong, not her.

She turned to him, that hard look in her eyes. "Oh, don't stop now. Believe me, I've been wondering for quite a while what you've been thinking."

Reece felt his back go up despite himself. He'd blown it—badly. Sarah had every right to be angry with him. But her words cut like knives, and he could feel himself beginning to bleed. It was too much when the wounds from losing Vanessa had barely scabbed over.

"Look, I said I was sorry. I couldn't deal after Van—"

She pulled the bottle out of the microwave, shot him a scathing look. "Well, so sorry the world didn't stop because Reece couldn't deal." She shook the bottle well, then squirted a few drops on her wrist before bringing it to the baby's mouth. "It must be nice to have that option."

It's—*her,* he reminded himself. *Her* cries stopped and she latched on to the bottle like it had been years since she'd last had food.

"She was my wife." He hated the need to justify himself.

"And she was my best friend. After Mike left, she was my only friend. Do you think you're the only one grieving for her?"

"It's not the same."

"No, it's not." She pulled the bottle out of the baby's mouth and pressed her to her shoulder, softly murmuring as she patted Rose's back. When the baby burped, she lowered her to the cradle of her arm and gave her the bottle again.

"It's not the same because I didn't shirk every responsibility I had. I didn't leave the woman carrying my child—as a favor to my wife and me—alone to deal with everything. I didn't abandon my baby when it was born, leaving her to my wife's best friend and surrogate to take care of. I didn't write my child out of my life like she was a mistake I couldn't face.

"So, you're right, it's not at all the same."

"I sent a check every month!"

"And that makes it okay?" The baby finished her bottle, so Sarah shifted her to her shoulder and crossed the kitchen. She opened the drawer near the refrigerator—a junk drawer judging by its contents— and pulled out an envelope.

"Is this how you soothe your conscience late at night? Is this how you put Rose out of your mind?" She flung the envelope at him. "Take your blood money. Take it and get the hell out of my house. I don't want it or anything else from you. Not now and definitely not in the future."

CHAPTER TWO

SARAH STORMED into the baby's room, where she laid Rose in her crib then promptly burst into tears. After turning on Rose's pink star mobile, so she'd have something to look at, Sarah sank to the floor, laid her head on her knees and sobbed like her heart was breaking all over again.

What was wrong with her? She'd sworn that she wouldn't do this. Had promised herself that she would encourage it when Reece took an interest in Rose. Had told herself she understood his pain. Understood why it had taken him so long to come around. Understood that he couldn't face the baby without facing everything that he'd lost.

She'd told herself all of that, had even believed it—until she had opened her front door to him. Rage had swept through her—rage like nothing she'd ever felt before, even when she'd found out Vanessa was dead. Not even having her husband leave her with two babies and almost no explanation had brought on this bone-deep fury.

How *dare* Reece show up like it hadn't been months since she'd last heard from him? How *dare* he throw money at her like that made his disinterest better? She'd needed him these past few months. Over and over again, she'd reached out to him for help, for company, for someone to share part of this burden with. And he had rebuffed her every single time.

It wasn't fair. She'd agreed to have this baby for Vanessa—and for Reece. Had agreed to be artificially inseminated, to become pregnant again so that she could give her best friend the baby Vanessa couldn't have. But Sarah hadn't signed on to go through the pregnancy alone. She hadn't signed on to juggle three children and a thriving Web-design business all on her own.

And she sure as hell hadn't thought that her entire life would change when this baby was born. From the moment she'd gotten pregnant, she'd thought of the baby as Vanessa's. That was the only way she could bring herself to give the newborn up. Even after Van died, she'd told herself that this was her best friend's baby. *Reece's* baby.

And when Vanessa Rose was born—named after her mother and grandmother—Sarah had distanced herself, sure that Reece would step up to the plate once he got himself together.

But days then weeks had passed and the only contact she'd had from Reece were those damned checks. She'd stopped calling him after Rose was four weeks old and by the time the baby was a month and a half old, she'd thought of Rose as hers. Not Reece's. Not even Vanessa's. But hers and Johnny's and Justin's.

The boys felt the same way. Though Rose annoyed

them—a lot—she wasn't "the baby" any longer. No, Johnny called her "my baby" or "our baby" and Justin told Sarah how much he loved having a baby sister. Sarah had opened her heart to this baby that was never meant to be hers. Had lulled herself into believing that Reece had written Rose off except for the money.

Reece's presence threatened their family unit, disrupted the bonds the four of them had formed. Reece and his criticisms reminded Sarah of the precarious position she was in. Rose didn't belong to Sarah and Johnny and Justin. Rose belonged to Reece. And at any moment he could snatch her away. Sarah knew her strength—honed from surviving the departures of a fair share of loved ones from her life—but she honestly doubted her ability to cope if Reece took Rose.

And why else would he have shown up here today, if not to claim his daughter? He'd probably woken up from his grief long enough to recognize Rose was the last link he had to Vanessa. So now he'd step in to be Rose's daddy with no thought to the impact that action would have on Sarah and her boys. Why couldn't Reece have stayed asleep and stayed away?

"Sarah?" Reece's voice sounded from the other side of the door. "Sarah, can I come in?"

The doorknob started to turn and she scrambled to slam the door in his face. "Not yet," she said, striving for a normal tone through the huskiness. "Give me a minute."

Wiping her hands across her eyes, over her nose, she struggled to make herself presentable. There was no way she could disguise the fact that she'd been crying, but she'd be damned if she greeted Reece with tears streaming down her face. She was stronger than that.

When she finally opened the door, her emotions were completely in hand. She even managed a brief smile. "I need to check on the boys."

"I just did." The smile he offered was tentative, barely present and nothing like the smiles Reece used to give her—before Vanessa's death. Those had been bright, excited, and so full of life she'd often wondered how his body could contain the joy he had for living.

"They're playing superheroes in their room."

Sarah glanced in the crib, and saw that her beautiful baby girl slept. "Come on, we can talk downstairs."

As she walked down the stairs, her behavior was wearing on her. How could she have talked to Reece— Reece, of all people—like that? He was the one person in the world who had loved Vanessa as much as she had. How could she blame him, then, if he loved her so much that he couldn't cope with anything after the accident?

There were no two ways around it—she owed the man an apology. And if it stuck in her craw, well then, that was too bad. She'd gotten herself into the mess by agreeing to be a surrogate mother to Vanessa and Reece's child. Now she would simply have to put on her big girl panties and deal with the fallout of a situation none of them had ever anticipated.

"Sarah." Reece stopped in the middle of the living room. "I'm so sor—"

"Please don't apologize. I'm the one who lost it." She

gestured to the sofa while she took a seat in the green-striped wingback chair Van had helped her pick out when she and Michael had first bought the house. It was as close as Sarah could get to an apology.

"I never intended for this to happen." His brown eyes were tortured when they met hers, the pain of losing his wife still fresh in them, despite the time that had passed. She recognized it, because her own pain was almost as fresh.

"Nobody thought Vanessa would die, Reece. It just happened."

"That's not what I meant." He shoved a hand through his hair as he stood to pace from one end of the room to the other. "At the funeral, I told myself all I needed was a little time. Some space to come to grips with losing Vanessa like that."

"I know—"

"No, you don't." The look he shot her was intense and full of self-loathing. "I was sure a few weeks would do it. But then two months passed, three. I picked up the phone to call you so many times, but there was nothing to say. Vanessa was what we'd always had in common and she was gone. I couldn't imagine bringing a baby into the world without her.

"So I let more time pass, told myself I'd face it when you went into labor. Let myself believe that I'd step up and do what I had to do once the baby was born. And then that day arrived."

He stopped in front of her, crouched next to her chair so they were at eye level. "I grabbed my coat, headed for the door, told myself I was ready to be a father. But that was a lie. I was nowhere near ready and all I could think about was that Vanessa should be with me. We should be going to the hospital together. We should be doing *all* of this together.

"I dropped my coat and keys on the floor, curled up on my couch and cried like a baby. When I woke up there was a message from you telling me I had a daughter. And I still couldn't make myself leave the room, still couldn't talk myself into going to the hospital. I couldn't pick up the baby—Vanessa's baby—and bring her home. Not without my wife."

Sarah swallowed against the lump in her throat as each word he spoke punched another little hole in her already leaky soul. He was in as bad shape as she was—worse, really.

Once again she asked herself how she could hold that against him. The answer was clear—she couldn't. And somehow, if he was ready to take Rose—her heart broke at the thought—she would find the strength to let the baby go and pretend it wasn't killing her.

He laid a hand on top of hers, which she'd tightly folded in her lap. "I am sorry, Sarah. I know these past few months must have been hell for you. I was a selfish bastard to let you go through them alone."

She shrugged, suddenly unable to berate him when he was doing such a good job of beating himself up. "It's done, Reece. We just have to find a way to go on from here."

"Do you think that's possible?" he asked.

"I don't think we've got a choice. You have a daughter who needs you and I—" Her voice broke despite her determination to keep it steady. "I have two sons who need their mother."

"And a daughter."

"What?" His words didn't make sense in the context of her grand, self-sacrificing speech.

"You have a daughter who needs you, too, Sarah."

Once more she had to swallow against the tightness in her throat. "Rose is yours, Reece. Yours and Vanessa's."

"And yours, Sarah." He lifted her hand, brought it to his lips. "She's yours most of all."

Reece watched as Sarah struggled to maintain her composure. A sick feeling rose up inside of him. "Did you think I'd come to take her from you? Is that what has you so upset?"

"I'd always planned on giving her to you and Vanessa, Reece. Even after Van died, I told myself Rose wasn't mine to keep—"

"Yet you're the only one who stuck by her through all of this. Do you really think I could forget that? You loved my daughter when I wasn't able to. What kind of a man would I be if I repaid that by ripping her away from the only mother she's ever known?"

She shook her head as she stared at him. "I don't understand. Where does that leave us?"

He said aloud the words he'd dreaded for the repercussion they'd have on his life. There was no going back, no retracting the commitment. His life was forever tied to this woman who fascinated him despite his best intentions otherwise. "Together, Sarah. All the rest are just details to be worked out. We're in this together now and I won't let you or Rose down ever again. I swear it."

IT WAS LATE the next afternoon before Reece had things arranged to his satisfaction at work. Sarah needed help and as the father of her child, he was the obvious choice. He couldn't leave the job completely—after all, there were bills to pay—but he could cut down on his hours and occasionally work from either his or Sarah's home.

It was time—past time—that he became a father to his daughter. The fact that he broke out in a cold sweat every time he so much as thought about Rose was of no consequence whatsoever.

And the fact that he hadn't been able to hold her yesterday—in truth, had barely been able to look at her—didn't matter, either. She was his responsibility and he would find a way to meet that, even if it killed him. He'd left Sarah and Rose on their own for too long.

"Hey, Reece, you got a minute?" He looked up to find Matt Jenkins, his partner for the past eight years, leaning against the doorjamb of Reece's office. With his faded jeans, tennis shoes and football jersey, Matt looked more like a college kid than an award-winning architect.

"Yeah, sure." Reece pushed aside the drawings he was working on, reached beneath the light table to turn it off.

"No, leave it on," Matt crossed the room in two long strides, his floppy red hair falling over one eye. "Is this the design for the Harbor account?"

Reece ran a hand over his tired eyes. He hadn't slept at all last night, his mind too full of his daughter, and Sarah, to allow him to drift into even the most uneasy of sleeps. He had no desire to discuss the intricacies of his newest building, not when all he really wanted was a bed and eight hours of sleep.

"Yo, earth to Reece."

"What?" Reece lowered his hands in time to see Matt staring at him with concern.

"Is this the Harbor account?"

"Yeah, it's coming together nicely."

Matt leaned over the light board. "How much do you have left to do?"

"I've got four sets of plans complete—including the outside design. They approved that this morning, so right now I'm working on the drawings for electric and plumbing."

Matt whistled, low and long. "I can't believe how fast this design has come together."

Reece snorted. "Yeah, well, when you've got no life it makes it easier to devote more time to work."

"That's why I stopped by. You want to go grab a beer, watch the game?"

"Game?"

His partner shook his head, even as he gestured to the jersey he had on. "The Cowboys, man. They're playing tonight."

"I can't."

"Reece—"

"Give it up, Matt." His voice was harsher than he'd intended, but all the emotions and uncertainties of the past few days welled up inside of him. "You need to figure out that I'm okay with not having a life right now."

"That's all going to change, though, isn't it, man? You're getting back on course, taking custody of your baby—"

"I didn't say I was taking custody of Rose."

Matt's eyes narrowed in confusion. "I thought that's what this whole work from home and cut down on the hours was supposed to be about?"

"It is. Sort of. I mean…"

"Hey, Reece, nobody blames you if you can't deal yet. This whole thing was Vanessa's idea, wasn't it? You weren't even sure you were ready for a baby when she was obsessing about it. And she's gone now, so why should you have to take responsibility for a kid you never really wanted?"

"Because she's *mine*. Because I helped create her, knowingly and willingly, and I can't walk away from that responsibility. I mean, look at Sarah. She agreed to the pregnancy with the understanding that as soon as the baby was born, she would be Vanessa's and mine. Instead, Sarah's been stuck caring for the baby for almost three months. Alone."

"That's what I'm saying. Maybe there's a reason for that. She's already a mom—"

"She's struggling, Matt. Seriously struggling. Are you suggesting I abandon her? I've been down that road and it hasn't worked out very well for either one of us."

"No, of course not. But why not think about adoption? She's already got two kids to handle on her own, you don't have a wife to take care of this baby. Maybe it'll be the best thing for both of you."

"No!" Outrage tinted everything with a red haze. "Rose is mine. I'm not giving her up to some stranger to raise."

"Whoa, sorry." Matt put his hands up, backed away. "I wasn't trying to cause problems. I just thought, since you were so conflicted about this whole thing—you and Sarah both—maybe it would be better for the kid to, you know, go to a family with a mom and dad who really wanted her and could devote the necessary time to raising her. I had no idea you felt so strongly about her."

"I don't. It's—" Reece stopped talking at the knowing look Matt shot him.

"No offense, bro. But for your sake and the sake of that little girl, I think you'd better figure out exactly what it is that you do feel—and what you want to do about it. You're moving in with her mom. You can say it's going to be totally platonic as often as you want, but you'll be sharing a house. Sharing a baby. Sharing everything. There are bound to be some issues."

"What kind of issues?" Reece asked, determined to play dumb and not admit his best friend had verbalized his deepest fear—and the source of more guilt than he wanted to think about.

Matt rolled his eyes, before shrugging into his prized Cowboys jacket. "Sexual issues, man. You're living in a house with a beautiful woman—"

"It's not like that." Surely that wasn't admiration for Sarah in Matt's voice?

Matt eyed him silently before saying in a subdued voice, "Isn't it?"

Reece flushed, felt his ears begin to burn. "Of course not. I just want to take care of Rose—"

"The two aren't mutually exclusive, you know."

"Sarah doesn't think of me like that. There's no way— What?"

"You said Sarah wasn't interested. You never said anything about yourself."

"My wife just died, man."

"I know that." Matt laid a bracing hand on his shoulder. "Which makes you doubly vulnerable right now—to Sarah and to Rose. Give a good, hard think about what you're doing here."

"I'm doing what's best for my daughter—and her mother."

"Yeah. But is it what's also best for you? I just don't want to see you get hurt. Or hurt Sarah."

Reece snorted. "Says the guy whose longest running relationship lasted all of five weeks."

Matt grinned, before heading for the door, "Which is why I know exactly what I'm talking about. So take my advice—" his expression turned serious "—and be careful."

HOURS LATER, Reece was still thinking about his friend's advice as he sat in his living room and half watched the Cowboys game Matt had been talking about. What *did* he want—besides helping Sarah out?

Matt's fears were groundless. Reece knew he and Sarah would never end up falling for each other. Despite the little sizzle he got whenever he saw her, Sarah was Vanessa's best friend and completely off-limits to him. And he knew she felt the same way. Their only connection would be Rose. Somehow he had to make amends for forcing Sarah to be the baby's sole caregiver.

He took a swig of his lukewarm beer. Hell, maybe Matt was right about the adoption thing. Maybe Reece should talk to Sarah about giving up Rose. He had no idea how to raise a baby, and she already had her hands more than full with the boys and her business. Logically, it made sense.

But everything inside of him rejected that course of action. She was Vanessa's daughter. Maybe not biologically, but in spirit she had been Vanessa's from the moment of her conception. Earlier, really.

He tried to ignore the pain as he'd been doing these past months. But tonight it wouldn't be denied. He reached behind him, picked up a picture of Van he had taken a few years ago. They'd been in Hawaii and had just finished windsurfing. She'd been tanned and happy and so beautiful he hadn't been able to resist snapping the picture. He'd also been the one to frame it and set it on the sofa table when they'd moved into this house.

He set the photo aside unable to bear looking at it—

at her. Doubling over in an effort to fight the agony, he lost his grip on the beer bottle and the glass shattered as soon as it hit the hardwood floor.

Shattered, like his marriage to Vanessa. Destroyed, like him without his wife. How had he gotten here? He waited for the familiar—and blessed—numbness to set in, but it wouldn't come. How had he gone from being on top of the world to having everything in his life turn to shit?

It was ironic really. Would be funny if it wasn't so terrible. His whole life he'd been afraid of failing, afraid of screwing up like his older brother had. His parents had spent years trying to get Brad on track, but nothing worked. So, instead of continuing to work with him, they'd written him off and turned all their hopes and dreams—all their attention—to Reece.

And he had never let them down. Had been afraid of what his failures would do to them after all the drugs and suspensions and misery they'd lived through from his brother. To compensate, Reece had been the golden boy. Good student, good athlete who grew up to have a good career and a good marriage. Everything they'd asked of him he'd done. Anything to avoid being the subject of his father's bitterness, of those angry, hurtful words.

And where had that effort gotten him? Sitting alone in his living room, drowning his sorrows and trying to figure out which way was up. The hell of it was, he had zero motivation to even try to make sense of his life, his future. It had taken every reserve he had to do right by

Sarah...and Rose. If he had his choice, he'd crawl away somewhere and never come out again.

But he couldn't do that. Not him, not Reece Sandler. His father's most recent lecture echoed in his head. Dropping out of society wasn't an option. *Hiding* wasn't an option. Reece had to keep going. Keep moving forward. Things would get better. They always did.

He cursed viciously. He had no idea how to make things better—not when he'd created such a colossal screw-up. With Vanessa, with Sarah, with Rose.

Rose. Before he could block it, an image of his daughter's little hands followed by images of her in Sarah's arms flashed into his head. She was beautiful, perfect—an interesting combination of him and Sarah. Strange that he'd never considered what she would look like, had never imagined parts of himself or Sarah on this baby. Rose had always been Vanessa's baby.

But Vanessa was dead. Rose would never know her, would never hear the voice or see the face of the woman who had set in motion the plan for Rose's very existence.

It was that thought, more than any other, that made up his mind for him. He owed it to his wife. Things might have been rocky the last few months of Vanessa's life—her unreasonable obsession with having a baby overshadowing all else—but that wasn't Rose's fault. Nor was it Sarah's.

As he bent to pick up the pieces of the shattered bottle, he knew for certain there would be no talk of adoption. He and Vanessa had made a commitment when they'd decided to have a child—to Sarah, to the baby, to themselves. And if he was afraid of screwing up at fatherhood, afraid of turning out like his old man, then he'd keep it to himself.

He'd honor the commitment they had made. Even if it destroyed him.

CHAPTER THREE

"SO, YOU'RE REALLY GOING to let him be a part of Rose's life?"

Sarah glanced up from her computer to find her six-foot-six "little" brother looming in her office doorway. "I have a doorbell, you know."

He held up his key ring. "And I have a key. That means I don't have to knock."

"That key is for emergencies only."

Tad laughed. "In this house, that's almost every day."

Too true. Sarah rubbed the back of her neck as she fought off a tension headache. Every day there was some new and exciting—or not-so-exciting—crisis to deal with. Hopefully Reece's presence would help change that, but she wasn't holding her breath. Part of her feared she was adding one more person to the house that would expect her to take care of him.

"So, are you?" Tad snatched a cookie off the plate she kept near her desk for Justin and Johnny, and downed it in two clean bites.

"Am I what?" Sarah answered absently, calculating all the things she still had to do before the day was over. She had a Web site to finish and debug, as she'd promised it to her client by the end of the week. The boys needed new shoes and she had to get to the grocery store—Rose was almost out of formula and the pantry was bare.

"Are you really going to let that jackass have anything to do with baby Rose?"

The virulence in her brother's tone snagged her attention like nothing else could have. "Reece is *not* a jackass."

"You could have fooled me. Any guy who leaves the mother of his child high and dry like he did you, ain't no prize."

"It's not like how you make it sound."

"No." Tad crowded closer, until he was in her face, his blue eyes blazing with a fury uncommon for her easygoing brother. "It's a hell of a lot worse than I made it sound and we both know it. I can't believe you're letting him into your lives after everything he's done."

Her headache ratcheted up a couple notches. She didn't need this, not now and not from Tad. She knew he was looking out for her—from childhood, he'd been the only constant in her life. But just because he'd stuck by her—just because they'd stuck by each other—didn't mean he got a major vote in how she lived her life now.

Besides, she was uncertain enough about this arrangement.

"It's not too late to tell him you changed your mind, Sarah. Hell, I'll tell him."

His gleeful tone sent her over the edge. "Do you have a better idea? Because if you do, then I'm all ears."

Whoa. Judging from the expression on Tad's face, that came out way too harsh. Taking a deep breath, she released it slowly as she rubbed her weary eyes. "Look, I'm sorry. I didn't mean to snap."

"No, you're right. This whole situation is a mess and you're trying to make the best of it." His tone was stiff, the camaraderie of a few minutes before gone.

"I wouldn't exactly call Rose a situation—or a mess." She wanted to soothe her brother's ruffled feathers, to make everything okay again, but she was nearly suffocating under the weight of everything she had to juggle, including her own fear and hurt.

"I didn't mean that, sis. I just meant—" He gestured as if trying to physically get the words out, his jerky movements indicating how on edge he was.

One of them had to make the first move to bridge this rift, so she pushed away from her desk and crossed to where Tad was half sitting, half lounging on her futon. She crouched beside him, and said, "I know you think I got a raw deal."

"I don't think. I know you—"

"And yes, Reece reacted badly. I'm not denying that. But he lost Vanessa. How would you feel if something happened to Pam?"

Tad actually winced at the mere suggestion of losing his wife.

"Exactly. So, after screaming at him like a crazy woman, I'm trying to cut him some slack."

She straightened and crossed to the door. "I got Rose out of the deal, and I wouldn't trade her for anything.

So the fact that Reece wants to change his life to fit with mine and the kids instead of ripping Rose away from us is a big plus in my mind."

"Yeah, but how do you know he isn't going to bolt at the first sign of trouble?" Tad demanded as he followed her to the kitchen.

Wasn't that the sixty-four-thousand-dollar question? And it was a fair question. After all, their father had pulled the exact same vanishing act on their mother when Sarah and Tad were young. They'd lived through their mother's nervous breakdown and subsequent emotional abandonment.

The truth was she didn't know that Reece was going to stick around. The one-two combination of what Mike had done to her when the boys were born and Reece's own MIA behavior reinforced the lessons from her parents. A part of her doubted Reece would be around for long.

Despite his behavior, she couldn't deny him this chance to bond with his daughter. He deserved that much. And as long as Sarah didn't get her hopes up, as long as she didn't start to count on him or expect him to be there for her, as long as she didn't let the boys get too close to him, then maybe the three of them could emerge from this with their hearts intact.

She said as much to Tad, then smiled as his eyes widened in surprise.

"You really aren't going into this blindly, are you?"

"Are you kidding me? Besides my very disastrous marriage to Mike, what have I ever gone into blindly?"

Her brother smirked. "Oh, I don't know. Surrogate motherhood?"

"That's different. That was for Vanessa."

"Yet you're still screwed."

"I am not screwed! I—"

"Okay, okay." He held his hands up in surrender. "I give up." He glanced at his watch. "I need to head home. I promised Pam I'd make dinner tonight and I've got to stop at the store and figure out what to make."

He leaned down and kissed the top of her head. "I'm not trying to be a jerk, you know. I don't want to see you get hurt again."

That was so Tad. He tormented her and antagonized her, but supported her and looked out for her all the while. How had she gotten so lucky? "Don't worry about it."

"Later, bro. Hey," she called as he walked out. "Fix that chicken breast thing with the spinach. You know Pam loves it."

A two-fingered salute was her only answer as Tad exited the side gate.

Sarah headed for the high cabinet above the stove where she kept her medicine. She shook out two Tylenol and swallowed them with a grimace. If she was going to get through this day, she needed all the help she could get.

No sooner had she settled herself in front of the computer to finish her work than the baby monitor on the corner of her desk went crazy.

Rose was awake.

REECE WIPED DAMP PALMS down the legs of his jeans for the third time in as many minutes. He was sitting in his car in front of Sarah's house trying to work up the nerve to ring the doorbell and see his child for the second time.

Vanessa's child.

Sarah's child.

Was he crazy, thinking this was going to work out? Thinking he could see Sarah every day and still successfully battle his guilt—over abandoning her and over the feelings he had for her that wouldn't go away? Thinking he could be a decent father to Rose?

Maybe he *was* insane, but it was too late for second thoughts. Too late to peel away from the curb. He'd never be able to live with himself if he took the easy way out.

With a deep breath for courage, he got out and walked slowly to the front door. No need to rush, after all, when he knew what lay on the other side of the door.

Or at least he thought he did. The door burst open before he'd taken the first step up to the porch and Johnny and Justin rushed out. "Uncle Reece, Uncle Reece, did you buy us something?"

"I sure did." He held up the bag from the toy store he'd stopped at before coming over. It was filled to the brim with stuff for the two boys. Sad to say there was only one thing in there for the baby—a soft, pink stuffed bunny that he hoped would go with the nursery.

He'd planned on buying more for little Rosie, lots more. But as he stared at the aisles of baby toys he'd realized he was woefully unprepared. Little boys he could handle, but baby girls were way out of his league.

He had no idea what toys she already had, didn't even know which toys—if any—would interest her. So he'd picked up the rabbit, hoping it would work and made a plan to talk to Sarah about providing anything else the baby might need.

"Really? What is it?" Johnny jumped up and down as he tried to peer inside the bag.

"Johnny Martin, get away from that bag this instant." Sarah's voice cut like a whip as she came to the door and he was relieved at how much better she looked than she had the other day.

She was still too thin, but it was obvious she'd gotten some sleep. Her short blond hair was washed and styled, her clothes actually fit—and looked good on her five-foot-ten frame—and the circles under her eyes looked less like bruises. She still looked different from the woman he'd known before all this had happened, but at least she was more recognizable now.

"You know better than to behave so rudely," she continued, staring her son down with a scowl Reece couldn't help but admire even as he battled against the familiar warmth working its way through him.

"But, Mom." Justin stuck up for his adored, older brother. "Uncle Reece promised there were presents for us."

"Oh, really?" She sent him an arch look over the boys' heads and Reece felt himself flush as if he were being scolded. "Well, let him in and we'll see what he brought you."

"Yeah! Come on, Uncle Reece. Come on." Johnny

did everything but get behind him and push him through the door.

"How was school today?" he asked the boys as he put the bag on the floor and kneeled next to it. Their little bodies were quivering with excitement and he had fun drawing out the moment.

"It was good. Our teacher's nice," Johnny answered impatiently.

"And were the two of you good?" he asked, reaching a hand inside the huge plastic bag, but not taking anything out of it. Yet.

"We're always good, Uncle Reece," Justin told him. "The teacher says we're very smart, but pre-pre—"

"Precocious," finished Johnny. "She tells Mom we're precocious. Whatever that means."

"It means you're lively," his mother said with a smile. "Perhaps a little too lively."

"Well, I guess that's a good enough report. For this." He pulled two giant dinosaurs out of the bag and watched as the boys' eyes lit with delight.

"A dinosaw, Mommy!" cried Justin happily. "A real dinosaw."

"Indeed." Sarah nodded. She was smiling, but Reece realized her eyes were wary. He was sorry for any concern his sudden reappearance was causing her, but he didn't know what else to do. It was past time for Sarah to have some help…and for little Rose to have a father.

He deliberately kept his eyes on the bag, refusing to look around the room for the baby. He'd work up to that slowly, give himself a few seconds to adjust to the idea of her before he actually had to interact with her. His heart was racing, his hands shaking, but he refused to give in to the fear. He would handle Vanessa's child and not turn into his father. He would not be overwhelmed by grief or inadequacy.

"I've got something else in here for you guys." He pulled out the Thomas the Tank Engine train set he hadn't been able to resist—along with the fifteen trains that would run on it.

Choruses of "Thomas" and "choo-choo" rang out for the next few minutes, interspersed with some pretty authentic-sounding dinosaur roars. When there was finally a lull in the noise level and all the toys had been opened, Sarah said, "Why don't you two take your new toys upstairs to play? I bet your dinosaurs would love to see your bedroom."

"Mom." Justin giggled as he climbed to his feet. "My dinosaur's not alive."

"It isn't?" she asked with mock disappointment. "I thought it was a real dinosaur."

"A real, *play* dinosaur," Johnny answered as he headed for the stairs. "Come on, Justin. Let's see if they can fit in our rocket launcher."

Reece watched them go with a grin. "Dinosaurs in space?"

Sarah laughed. "Something like that." She studied him for a minute. "You came back."

Tension filled the room, so thick he was sure he could breathe it in. "I said I would."

"I know you did." Her lips twisted into a little smirk

that told him his word wasn't worth much. Which kind of ticked him off, even as he told himself his behavior for the past several months had given her a pretty sound basis for her opinion.

"Look, Sarah, I screwed up." He wasn't sure where the words were coming from, but he knew he had to say them. Get them out, so that they could move on. "I'm sorry. You have no idea how sorry I am. But I'm here now and I'll do better. I won't leave you—" he swallowed the bile rising in his throat "—you or Rose hanging again. You have my word on that."

Sarah studied him for a minute, her blue eyes more intense than he'd ever seen them. Was she finally going to let him in? Finally going to trust him. Then, just when his nerves were stretched to the breaking point, she opened her mouth to say something and he felt his stomach tighten in anticipation.

But Rose chose that moment to begin crying and Sarah's response was lost in her rush to comfort the baby. His lungs tightened in his chest, frozen so that the act of breathing was nearly an Olympic event. His daughter was crying. *His* daughter.

"Do you want to hold her while I fix her bottle?" Sarah glanced over her shoulder at him as she lifted the baby from the swing.

It was a test. But knowing that did nothing to prevent his hands from growing damp or his breath from hitching. What if he hurt the baby somehow? What if he dropped her? She was so small.

His hesitation must have registered, because Sarah's smile faded. "Never mind. I've got her."

"No. I want to hold her. I just—"

"Just what?"

"I don't know how." It grated to admit to what was yet another failure, but what was his pride worth when the alternative was unwittingly hurting his child?

She stared at him in disbelief. "You've never held a baby?"

"Not one that small."

After studying him for a minute, she nodded as if she'd made some kind of decision. "Okay. Sit on the couch and I'll hand her to you."

"All right." He sat as Sarah and Rose came closer. Everything narrowed to this one moment, each of his senses perfectly tuned to his daughter and her mother.

Sarah laid Rose gently in his arms and the sweet scent of baby powder tickled his nose. She was a soft, warm weight, barely more than a sack of groceries or one of his design books.

She'd stopped crying the second Sarah had handed her to him and now stared at him with big, blue eyes as if she was as curious about him as he was about her.

"Watch her head," Sarah cautioned, and instantly he shot his elbow up so that his forearm lent support to the baby's neck. One tiny fist flailed around before being tucked inside that rosebud pink mouth. His heart melted into a soft, runny puddle in his chest.

This was his child. His daughter. His beautiful baby girl. He could barely take it in. His eyes burned and he closed them for a minute, swallowing hard in an effort to keep from making a fool of himself in front of Sarah.

She must have understood, though, because he felt a gentle hand on his shoulder as she murmured, "I'll go get that bottle now."

Then she was gone and he was alone with his little girl for the first time in his life. "Hey there, little Rosie," he whispered. "How's my girl? How's Daddy's best little girl?" Her eyes widened and she stared at him, as if trying to determine if the voice she'd heard had come from him.

"That's right, baby. Your daddy's talking to you. Yes, I am." Instinctively, he bounced her gently in the cradle of his arms, just enough to soothe but not startle. "I'm sorry I haven't been here before, but I'm here now. And I'm not going anywhere."

He leaned down and nuzzled her cheek with his nose. "No, I'm not. Daddy's learned his lesson. Yes, he has. You're my own darling girl and I won't ever leave you again."

"Here's her bottle." Sarah's voice sounded tight as she stood over him, the bottle in her hand.

His stomach dropped to his toes. "You want me to feed her?"

"Well, you are her father, aren't you?"

"Yeah, but—I don't know how to feed a baby. What if I choke her or—"

"You'll do fine. Tilt your left elbow up slightly so her head is a little more elevated." He did as she told him. "Perfect."

"Now what?" He knew he sounded panicked, but couldn't help it. He *was* panicked. He couldn't do this. He wasn't ready for—

Sarah didn't give him a choice. She simply popped the bottle into the baby's waiting mouth, then gestured for him to take it.

"See, nothing to it." Sarah settled into the chair opposite him.

Easy for her to say. She wasn't the one running very rusty knowledge of infant CPR through her head. What would he do if the baby choked?

Despite his panic, everything worked fine. The baby sucked and swallowed, sucked and swallowed in a cute rhythm, her eyes growing heavier by the second.

He was starting to relax, to get into the groove of feeding her when Sarah said, "Okay, that's enough."

"But she only took half the bottle."

"She needs to be burped. Then you can feed her the rest."

His heart froze all over again. "Burped?"

"Yep." Sarah reached over and laid a receiving blanket across his chest and shoulder. "Just shift her up a little and rub her back. She's pretty good at it."

"Shift her?" Clamping down on the instinctive panic, he reminded himself men all over the world did this every day. Surely he could manage one burping session.

It wasn't fast and it wasn't pretty, but eventually he got Rosie positioned where he thought she needed to be. He rubbed her back in soothing circles, but nothing happened.

Finally, he looked at Sarah in frustration and demanded, "What am I doing wrong?"

"Nothing. But maybe try shifting her a little higher on your shoulder?"

Higher? Was she insane? Much higher and Rosie would be in nosebleed territory. But he did what Sarah suggested—what choice did he have, really?—and was rewarded with a big burp. Few things in his life had ever felt as satisfying.

"Okay, she should be ready for the rest of the bottle now."

Sweat rolled down his spine. He was going to have to move Rose again. Nodding, slowly, he began the torturous process of returning her to a proper feeding position. But by the time he got her down to the crook of his elbow again—with nary a head bobble in sight—her eyes were closed and her chest was rising and falling in a surprisingly rapid rhythm. "Is she okay?" he asked.

"She's fine," Sarah said. "Babies have a much faster respiration than adults."

"Obviously." He stared at his daughter, awe and love and more than a little fear filling his heart until it nearly burst from his chest. He counted her fingers, admired her long, black eyelashes and chubby, pink cheeks.

"What do I do now?" he asked, when there was nothing else to look at, nothing else to catalog.

"I'll put her upstairs in her crib."

"Okay." He looked into Sarah's wary eyes, grinned in an effort to put her at ease. "And then we can talk?"

"Yes, Reece." Her voice was nowhere near as enthusiastic as his. "Then we'll talk."

She was back before he was ready and Reece felt his carefully planned speech dissolve into nothingness. How did he tell Sarah what he wanted? How did he broach a subject so sticky, so final? Everything he'd thought of yesterday and this morning sounded like meaningless platitudes, but nothing else was coming to him.

"You want to take Rose, don't you?"

His startled gaze met hers. "No, Sarah. Of course not. I thought we'd settled that two days ago."

Her arms were crossed over her chest, her lips tight. "Well, what do you want, then?"

"I want to be a part of her life. A part of your life and the boys'."

"You want visitation rights?"

He sighed, ran a hand through his hair as he struggled, again, for the right way to bring up what he did want. "Not exactly."

"Partial custody?"

"I've spent the past two days thinking about nothing but this and I really believe I've hit on the best way to handle this whole situation." He swallowed over the lump in his throat, then bit the bullet. "I want to move in with you."

CHAPTER FOUR

SARAH KNEW SHE WAS DOING a darn good impression of a flycatcher, but try as she might, she couldn't seem to close her mouth—any more than she could force words through the tight lump in her throat. A lump that was growing tighter, and bigger, with every strangled breath.

But Reece was staring at her, his dark chocolate eyes half-amused and all concerned. Almost as if he had really said what she'd thought he said. But surely—

Her knees threatened to buckle, so Sarah grabbed onto a nearby chair. Focused on how it felt beneath her unsteady palm. Concentrated on her breathing. In, out. In, out. Again and again she repeated the process until the buzzing in her ears receded.

"Move in?" It took everything she had to force the half-strangled words through her tight throat. "You want to move in? Here? With me?"

"I do." Reece nodded, his expression slowly relaxing now that she was stringing words together in a semi-coherent fashion.

"Why?"

He raised an eyebrow, as if shocked that she had to ask. But at this point, Sarah wasn't taking anything for granted. Four days ago she hadn't been able to get the man to acknowledge that baby Rose existed and now he was talking about becoming a permanent fixture—not only in Rose's life, but in Sarah's and her sons', as well.

"I thought that would be obvious, Sarah. It's the perfect solution."

Her back went up at the condescension in his tone, even as she told herself she wasn't being fair. She'd known Reece a long time and he'd never once treated her as anything less than an equal. Maybe it was her own issues that were making her take such affront at his words—and tone. It had been six years since she'd had a man living in this house, and based on how badly that had gone, she was less than keen to repeat the experience.

"What exactly is it the solution to, Reece?" Memories of her marriage gave her words more bite than she had intended.

"Well, it's obvious you need help." He glanced around the house as if it was one small step from being condemned. "I could—"

"I do not need your help." He'd hit her hot button and the explosion she'd felt welling up inside of her detonated before she could even try to stop it. For the three years she'd been married to Mike, she'd had to put up with being told how incompetent she was. How she needed him to do things for her. How she wouldn't survive without him.

She'd tolerated that because marriage had represented security and after the farce of her childhood, she'd clung to any and all she could find. But she wasn't that woman anymore. Hadn't been since the day Mike walked out on her and she'd realized she was better off without him. For Reece—for anyone—to try to cast her back in that role was untenable.

"I'm sorry if my house isn't up to your standards, but I am doing the best I can here. I don't need a big, strong man around—"

"I never said you did." He shoved a hand through his hair in frustration, a familiar gesture from when Vanessa was alive. "But I want to be a part of Rose's life, a real part."

"What's wrong with regular weekly visitations like noncustodial parents?"

"Because we aren't like those other people. Because this isn't a case of us being divorced. Or even involved." He sighed, extended a hand out to her. For one long moment, she wanted to take it—to feel the strength and warmth and concern that she knew his touch would communicate.

But it wouldn't pay to count on him. His behavior in the past few months certainly hadn't demonstrated reliability or dependability.

"I don't understand." Because she still wanted to reach for him, Sarah rubbed her hands up her suddenly cold arms. "Why the sudden change of heart?"

She could almost hear his teeth grind in frustration. "I want to help you. To be a full-time part of Rose's life."

"For how long?" The words were out before she could censor them.

"Can't you trust me at all?" he asked. "I know I screwed up—badly. But I want to make that up to you. And to my daughter."

Sarah closed her eyes as pain flooded her, so sharp that she almost glanced down to see if she was bleeding. Why had she ever wanted Reece to be a part of Rose's life? Why had she ever thought she could give her beautiful baby up?

But she wasn't giving Rose up. Sarah was only sharing Rose…with her father. Still, it was so much harder than Sarah had expected it to be, this having to share the responsibility for someone she'd come to think of as exclusively hers.

With a sigh, she sank onto the sofa that had seen better days. The boys had jumped on it so much that the springs had broken, leaving the middle sagging badly. When she'd been pregnant with Rose, she had had to actually roll off the couch if she was unfortunate enough to sit on it before remembering to pick an end.

Keep an open mind, she reminded herself, as she stared at her best friend's husband. For the first time, she noted the lines of strain around his eyes, the dark circles that—while nowhere near as dark as her own— heralded more than a few sleepless nights. They didn't make him any less attractive, but they did lessen her anger.

Sympathy welled before she could stop it. Everything was changing, yes, but she wasn't the only one in a state of flux. Reece had lost his wife and gained a baby that came with a different mother already attached. Was it any wonder he appeared stressed?

And Sarah was only making it more difficult for him.

With a sigh, she counted backward from twenty. Then aimed for a calm, rational, grown-up voice and said, "Why don't you tell me why moving in here is the perfect solution?"

He didn't respond immediately. And just when she thought he wouldn't, he said, "First, why don't you tell me what you object to?"

What did she object to? Was he kidding? Where did he want her to start? With the fact that she'd been getting along fine without a man for years now?

"What will people think?"

It was lowest on her list of objections, but seemed the easiest to discuss without digging through her baggage. Besides, it was true. She'd put up with more than enough talk when she'd shown up pregnant without a man around. She could only imagine what the neighbors would say about her shacking up with her best friend's husband.

"That's it?" he asked incredulously. "That's your big objection?"

"No!" She jumped up and started to pace. "But it's one of them. Right next to my worry about what this will do to the boys."

"What do you mean?"

He looked so clueless. How could he talk about disrupting her whole life—the boys' whole lives—and not even think about the consequences.

"Johnny and Justin are old enough to figure things out, Reece." She closed her eyes, prayed that he would understand what she was saying without her actually having to form the words. "They're old enough to want things that other kids have."

"Like what?"

"They want a father, Reece. Mike cut out before they were born, and they don't understand why they don't have a dad when other kids do. They ask about him and though I do my best to be both mom and dad, it's not enough. If you move in here, it's only a matter of time before they get attached to you. Too attached."

She saw the awareness dawn in his eyes, the realization that when he'd come up with this ridiculous scheme, he had only taken into account his and Rose's best interests. Wasn't that typical?

"If we talk to them, explain—"

"They turned five two weeks ago, Reece. How on earth can I explain this to them when I don't even understand it myself? Oh, by the way, boys, Uncle Reece is going to be living here. But don't get too attached—it's only short-term."

She laughed, to hide the sobs that threatened to escape. "They don't even know what short-term is."

"I didn't say anything about it being short-term, Sarah." Reece stood, crossed the room until he was right in front of her. Tension vibrated between them, sharp and real. "If we do this, it's for the long haul."

She felt the blood drain from her face. "What do you mean?"

"I mean, it's the best solution for everyone. Rose and Justin and Johnny need a male influence around the house. You need someone to help shoulder the responsibility—and the bills."

Her spine straightened so quickly that it was actually painful. But she fought the affront. "And what do you need, Reece? What do you get out of this?"

WHAT DID HE GET OUT OF THIS? Where did he start? A chance to be near his daughter, a chance to watch her grow. The opportunity to be a part of a real family so he wouldn't be so alone.

But how did he say that to this woman, for whom his feelings had exceeded the bonds of friendship for more years than he ever let himself acknowledge? This woman who had worked so hard to include him? How did he admit to the days and weeks and months of self-imposed loneliness without sounding like a total loser? Or a total user?

He considered dodging the question. But Sarah was staring at him. And suddenly it wasn't so hard to tell the truth—or at least part of the truth.

"I get a chance to be with my daughter. To be with you and the boys. To have someone to take care of for a change."

"I don't need a white knight. I can take care of myself—and my children—on my own."

He wanted to protest, to look around at the total disaster that was her house. To put her in front of a mirror and force her to see what he saw—a woman on the brink of sheer and total exhaustion.

But that was the quickest way to get himself kicked out. Oh, Sarah wouldn't stop him from seeing the baby, but visits would be restricted to an hour here or there. An afternoon. Maybe one night a week. And that wasn't what he wanted—not now that he'd held his daughter in his arms. He wanted everything. And his proposal, unorthodox as it was, really was the best solution.

He wanted to say all that to Sarah. To tell her to trust him. To promise that he wouldn't let her down. But hell, he had no right to make those promises— and she wouldn't believe them anyway. Not with his track record.

But that would stop here, stop now, if she let it. If she would give him a chance—

"What other objections do you have?" His voice was harsher, more abrupt, than he would have liked. He could feel everything—Rose, Sarah, his entire family— slipping away from him and it made him harsh. Desperate.

"How would it work?" She waved a hand around the room. "In case you haven't noticed, we're pretty much at capacity around here as it is. Where would you put your stuff? Where would you stay?"

"You have a guest room, right?"

"Yeah." Her doubtful look spoke volumes about

what she thought of his ability to fit everything he'd need into that one small room.

"For now, I don't need much. Just a bed and a place to put my desk and drafting table."

"Drafting table? You want to work here, too?"

He had to bite the inside of his cheek to keep from smiling at her absolute incredulity. "Well, of course. I won't be much help if I'm always at the office."

For long moments, she didn't say anything. Just watched him with those blue eyes that seemed to see all the way to his soul.

Finally, when his nerves were stretched to the breaking point and nausea churned in his stomach, she spoke. "I already work here. We can't both be in the house all the time. We'd kill each other."

He couldn't help the smile that sprang to his lips. "Somehow, I doubt that. But I'm not talking all the time. I figured I'd work part-time here and part-time at the office."

"When?"

"I don't know. That's something we'll have to work out. I can be here during your busiest times, helping out with the kids, and—"

"No offense, Reece, but I don't need someone else to take care of."

"I don't need anyone to take care of me. I've been managing for most of my adult life. It's not like Vanessa was the homemaking type."

They both froze at the mention of his dead wife, and he cursed himself. Things hadn't exactly been going swimmingly, but at least he and Sarah had been conversing. Now, the mere mention of Vanessa seemed to have shattered whatever accord they'd achieved.

Exasperated, he walked to stand near the window. The boys scampered around the backyard with bug nets and jars. Watching them, the frozen mass inside of Reece began to soften. It wasn't a full-out thaw, but there was a definite melt in the region of his heart. It was all he could do to keep from laughing as Justin tripped over Johnny's net and sprawled in the grass, his own net landing, incongruously, over his face.

"They need a male influence, Sarah." He nodded toward the boys, who tumbled over each other.

"I know that." Her voice was sharper and more abrupt than it had been.

"I'm not criticizing you." He grabbed her arm and pulled her to the window. "You've done a fabulous job. But you've done it alone and that's not fair—to you or them.

"Look at them. They're fabulous boys. Smart and curious and complete troublemakers. Don't you think it's time you let someone help you with them?"

"I've survived this long."

"Surviving isn't living, you know."

"Said the kettle to the pot."

"Exactly. I've spent the past seven months hiding from reality, pretending my wife isn't dead and my life isn't shattered. It's gotten me nowhere."

"It's not the same thing—"

"I'm not saying it is. But, Sarah—" He held her ice-

cold hand in his warm one, tried desperately to think of
what he could say to change her mind. "I need to do this.
I need to be here—for Rose and for you. And for those
boys."

Her eyes searched his and he wished he knew what
she was looking for. He'd give it to her in a heartbeat.
Less. Because he was smart enough to know that, right
now, neither one of them could make it on their own.

"I guess we could give it a trial run," she said, her
voice sounding reluctant. "A couple of weeks to see
how things are working—"

"Two months. We need at least two months to be able
to make any real decisions."

"That's way too long. We might kill each other in
that time."

"I don't think so. Besides, how will we be able to tell
if it's going to work if we don't give it our best shot?"

"One month," she countered firmly. "And that's my
best offer. If, after four weeks, things aren't going like
we hoped, you move out. No harm, no foul."

He fought the urge to shout and thrust a fist into the
air in victory. "One month sounds perfect."

"And we need some rules."

"Of course we do." His mind raced ahead to what
he'd need to pack to make the move.

"I'm serious."

"So am I."

"No, you're not. You're not even listening to me."

"Of course I am. We need to make—um." His mind
went blank.

"Rules, Reece. We need to make rules."

"All right, if you say so. What kind of rules are we talking about?"

"Everybody is responsible for him or herself."

"Everybody?" He raised an eyebrow.

"Except the children, obviously. I don't want to have to clean up after you, do your laundry, that kind of thing."

"I'm not a child," he reminded her. "I've been taking care of myself for a long time now."

"And no women."

"Excuse me?"

"I don't care what you do when you're not in this house, but you can't bring overnight guests home."

His stomach churned and for the first time since he'd come up with this plan, he had serious doubts. Did Sarah not know him at all? "Sarah, my wife just died. I'm not out searching for female companionship."

Her color rose, but she refused to back down. "Not now, no. But suppose this thing works out? Suppose you don't move out after a month? Eventually you'll want to date again—and that's completely your business. But I don't want you to bring your dates here to—"

"That won't be a problem." She winced at his tone, but shit, what was he supposed to say? He hadn't looked at another woman since Vanessa had died, and he resented, like hell, Sarah's implication that he couldn't keep it zipped.

But was it fair to resent her? Maybe he hadn't been as good at hiding his response to her as he'd thought.

Maybe, despite his best intentions, she'd noticed the attraction he secretly felt for her.

Finally, she nodded. "Okay, then."

"Okay, what?"

"Okay, when can you move in?"

He grinned, elation sweeping away all irritation like it had never been. "I thought you'd never ask."

CHAPTER FIVE

SARAH WATCHED in horror as Reece made yet another trip to the big maroon truck he'd pulled into her driveway an hour before. *All I need is a bed and room for my desk and drafting table.*

She'd been a fool to believe him. He'd already made six trips upstairs—and she had made four. She'd probably still be carrying boxes if Rose hadn't woken up and demanded her afternoon snack.

The bottle shifted in the baby's mouth and Rose let out a startled cry. "Shh, my darling," Sarah murmured as she repositioned the baby. "Mama's got you. Mama's got you."

The words no longer felt foreign and the guilt had receded, even if it hadn't disappeared completely. While she still lay awake some nights, staring at the ceiling and wondering at the quirks of fate that had brought her to this place, she was coming to understand that she couldn't spend her life feeling guilty that she had lived and Vanessa had died. That she could have children and her best friend couldn't.

Nor could Sarah change the fact that Rose needed a

mother to take care of her—and that she, Sarah, was that mother.

"This is the last trip," Reece called on his way out the door.

"I'll believe that when I see it," Sarah muttered.

"I heard that." His voice echoed through the open door.

"Good." She tried her best not to notice how good he looked in his jeans and T-shirt, his muscles taut and hard as he carried in another box. He was Vanessa's husband and it was wrong—so wrong—for Sarah to notice how attractive he was.

"Mommy?"

Sarah turned to find Johnny staring at her with wide, serious eyes. The expression was so out of place on his face that it took her a minute to realize that he was worried. "What's the matter, precious?" She balanced Rose's bottle between her chest and chin for a moment, using her free hand to pat the couch next to her. "And where's your brother?"

"Justin is looking at Uncle Reece's truck. He likes trucks."

Justin liking trucks was an understatement if she'd ever heard one. "I thought you liked trucks, too."

"I do. It's just—"

"Just what?"

"Is Uncle Reece going to stay with us? Forever?"

Her heart dropped to her toes. This was what she'd been worried about—Justin and Johnny not adjusting to Reece being here. Or adjusting too well. Both situations were fraught with pitfalls and the capacity for her boys to be hurt.

She cuddled Johnny against her. "I don't know about forever, sweetheart. But he'll be with us for a while."

"Oh." The monosyllabic reply didn't tell her much in terms of what he was thinking or feeling so she waited for him to say more.

When he didn't, she smoothed a hand over his still-soft, baby-fine hair and asked, "Is that okay with you?"

"I guess."

"You guess? That's not a very good answer, you know."

"I know. But Todd's dad stays with them all the time. I just thought maybe Uncle Reece could be like that."

"Yes, honey, but Uncle Reece isn't your father. You know that."

"He's Rose's father." Johnny's face scrunched up, as if he was deep in thought. "Right?"

"Right," she answered cautiously.

"So why can't he be our father, too? Justin and I talked it over and we think he'd be a great dad."

She actually felt the explosion from that bomb in every cell of her being. Why had Mike walked away before the boys had ever gotten the chance to know him?

Because she'd picked a total loser for a husband, that was why.

Why had she ever agreed to this ridiculous setup? Why had Vanessa died and put her in this position? And what on earth was she supposed to tell the boys—now and later?

Her mind searched for an answer, but she didn't

know what to say. How could she hope to explain something to his five-year-old satisfaction that she really didn't understand herself?

But how could she not?

"I can't be your dad, Johnny, because I'm your uncle." Reece stood nearby, his hand on Justin's shoulder. Her second son was listening just as hard as his brother, trying to make sense of the bizarre situation.

"And because you already have a dad." Reece reached a hand out and Johnny put his in it without hesitation. "But that doesn't mean I can't do a lot of the things with you that a dad might."

"Like what?" Justin asked, a trace of suspicion in his voice.

"Like push you on the swings at the park or play hide-and-seek or build your train set."

"Mom already does all that." Justin's voice went from suspicious to scornful in the blink of an eye.

"Well, that's true." Crouching, Reece took his time looking both of her sons in the eye. "So what is it you want me to do with you?"

"Take us to McDonald's!" Johnny shouted, as if the answer was the most obvious one in the world.

"And teach us to play baseball. Mom can't hit the ball no matter what she does."

Sarah swallowed the lump in her throat as she was reminded yet again, how lucky she was to have the boys—despite their proclivity for trouble. "Well, maybe if you threw the ball at me instead of the ground, I wouldn't have such a hard time hitting it."

"Whatever," scoffed Justin. "You don't know how to hold the bat, Mom."

"I would love to teach you to play baseball and soccer and anything else you want to learn," Reece said. "And I wouldn't mind some chicken nuggets right about now, myself." He glanced at Sarah. "If it's okay with your mom, maybe we could head there for dinner?"

"We could probably arrange that." She stepped forward, Rose balanced against her shoulder, and ruffled both boys' hair in turn. "Why don't you run and get your shoes while I pack a bottle for the baby."

"Okay!" yelled Justin, as he ran for the stairs.

"Cool." Johnny scrambled after his brother.

Sarah watched them go with an indulgent smile, then turned to Reece. A completely unfamiliar warmth spread though her as their eyes connected, an awareness of Reece as more than her best friend's husband or her baby's father.

As her breath hitched in her chest she realized— with some shock—that she was looking at Reece as a man. As a very attractive man. A man she wanted to get up close and personal with.

Clasping Rose to her chest, she stumbled back. "I'll just go get the baby bag ready," she muttered.

"Do you want me to hold Rose?"

No! She wanted him to go upstairs, collect his stuff and walk out the door while she still remembered he was Van's husband and off-limits.

But all she said was, "Sure," as she peeled the baby from her chest.

"Sure." He took his daughter gingerly. The handoff took half the time the last one had. He had gotten so much better with Rose in such a short time that it made her stomach hurt.

Of course, it could be the guilt eating away at her stomach lining. How could she have responded to him like that, even for a second? Vanessa was probably rolling in her grave and Sarah couldn't blame her. He was her best friend's husband. Vanessa's husband.

It didn't mean anything, she assured herself as she mixed up a bottle of formula. Reece was a hot guy and she—she hadn't been that close to a man in more years than she cared to contemplate. Of course her body had reacted—it didn't mean her heart had. Or her head.

No, the warmth she'd felt when their gazes had connected had been purely physical. The same with the jolt that came when his hand brushed hers as he reached for Rose. It didn't mean anything. She wouldn't let it.

She slid the bottle into the diaper bag, then filled a second one with water. No, there would be nothing beyond parenting between them. It was a good thing that Reece was getting to know Rose, a good thing that he was involved in her life. Wasn't that what Sarah had wanted all along?

Be careful what you wish for…. The old adage echoed as Sarah recalled the conversation she'd had the night before with her brother.

"Are you sure you want to do this, Sarah?" Tad had asked as he fixed the wobbly slats on the playset she'd bought for the boys last year.

"I think Reece is right. It's the best solution to the problem."

The look her brother shot her told her he thought she was insane. "Moving a man you barely know into the house with you is the best solution? For who?"

"I've known Reece for years, Tad. He would never do what you're implying."

"Maybe not, but you can't be too careful in today's age."

"You're being ridiculous."

She'd started to brush past him, to go into the house and check on Rose, but he grabbed her hand, effectively stopping her. "What if he's just here to use you? To get to know Rose then take her from you. He could find any number of things to lie about while he's staying here, in an effort to prove you're an unfit mother."

She hadn't had an answer to Tad's question last night. And despite thinking of little else in the past twenty-four hours, she still didn't. But she was afraid, in a way she'd never been when Reece wasn't interested in Rose.

Typical of her life, wasn't it? She'd thought she'd wanted Reece to take an active role. For a little while she had actually wanted him to take custody of Rose so that Sarah could go back to the semi crazed status of her regular life. But now the thought of giving up her sweet baby girl hurt worse than anything she'd ever experienced—even coping with pregnancy and the twins on her own after Mike had decided to "follow his bliss."

When Reece left—and he would leave, of that Sarah

was sure—how devastating would it be? One day when the boys got on his nerves or work became more important than home or he realized that he didn't need Sarah to help him care for Rose, he would walk out. Leave her and the boys. Just like Mike had. Just like her father had. Just like her mother had, in her own way. And Sarah would be left to pick up the pieces. Again.

"Mom! What's taking so long? I'm starving!" Justin clutched his tummy dramatically.

"That's all part of my evil plan," she answered, shaking off her worries so that he wouldn't see she was upset. Even at five, he was uncannily perceptive when it came to her moods.

"What evil plan?" asked Reece, as he followed Johnny into the kitchen.

"The one where I starve them so that when I give them vegetables they'll eat them all!" She let out the witch's cackle the boys got such a kick out of.

"Silly, Mom! There's no vegetables at McDonald's," Justin said.

"No vegetables?" She paused dramatically. 'Then I don't think we should go. If they don't have broccoli, I don't think it's the place for us."

"Mom." Johnny groaned. "Come on! I want chicken nuggets."

"Chicken nuggets?" She lifted her eyebrows.

"Yeah. And French fries. And a vanilla milk shake," Justin said.

"A milk shake, too?" She gaped. "I don't think those little tummies will hold all that food."

"Sure they will," Justin answered. "I told you, I'm starving."

Sarah sighed. "Well, I suppose, just this one time…"

The boys cheered then ran for the door. "Don't worry, Uncle Reece," Johnny called over his shoulder. "Mom always says that, but she doesn't mean it."

"She doesn't, huh?"

"Nope. We always get a milk shake when we go to McDonalds."

"Isn't that a coincidence?" Reece asked, shooting her a grin before following her children. "So do I."

Sarah gathered her purse and the baby bag. She might have her doubts about Reece—and his staying power—but there was no law that said she couldn't enjoy whatever time she and the boys had with him. She would just have to remind Justin and Johnny that this was temporary, and pray that they understood. Because if Reece hurt her kids, she'd never forgive him. Or herself.

REECE STARED at Sarah as she juggled feeding the baby and opening Justin's ketchup pack while discussing which video game was really the best with Johnny.

"Obviously, it's Action Heroes, Mom," Johnny said. "You just don't know that 'cuz you're a girl."

"Oh, really?" She reached for the barbecue sauce and opened that, too. "I still say the pilot one. He can fly, after all."

"But that's only a plane, Mom." Justin joined in the argument. "The action heroes really can do all those things without machines. 'Cuz of their special powers."

Sarah winked at Reece as she considered the boys' arguments. "You know, that's a pretty good point. Maybe you're right. Maybe that Action Heroes game really is the best."

"Yeah!" Justin and Johnny chorused. "So does that mean we can get it for Christmas this year?"

"You've still got three months until Christmas. Don't you want to wait until it's a little closer to make your decision?"

"No way. It's the coolest game ever."

"All right, then. Action Heroes it is. But I do have a request. If your action figures really are the coolest, then I bet they would appreciate not being flushed down the toilet anymore. I know I would certainly appreciate not having to fish them out."

Reece almost laughed out loud as the boys took an inordinate amount of time to consider their mother's request.

"All right," Johnny finally said with a sigh. "We'll stop trying to bury them at sea."

"I'm so glad to hear that." She shifted Rose to her shoulder and began to pat the baby gently on her back. "Now eat your food so you can spend a few minutes on the playscape."

"Yay!" The disappointment of not being able to flush their favorite toys was buried by the prospect of something even more exciting to do.

Forcing himself to stop chewing and swallow, Reece shifted his gaze from Sarah's sparkling face. He would banish this unwitting attraction. Now that he was on the road to having everything he wanted, there was no way he was going to screw things up by hitting on Sarah. That wasn't parenting or supporting her. Somehow acting on this desire seemed worse than abandoning her for so long. Any further along this path and he'd prove himself to be as bad a father as his own had been. Worse maybe, because at least his dad had shown up at the dinner table every night. He might have bitched and moaned through the entire meal, but at least he'd been there.

As Reece watched the boys scarf down their food in record time, he couldn't help smiling. And though he was being careful not to look at his wife's best friend, Sarah must have seen his grin, because she murmured, "Amazing what a little motivation can do, isn't it?"

"You can say that again." He paused for a moment. "I'm sorry, Sarah. More sorry than I can say. I was a total ass."

"Reece—"

"No, let me say this. I can't change what happened, but I can promise you that it won't happen again. I'll never walk away from my daughter."

Sarah watched him, tension evident in every line of her body. Excruciatingly long seconds ticked by as he waited for her response. Finally, she smiled. Not one of those brief, trying-to-be-polite smiles that he'd been getting for days now. No, this was a full-fledged, thousand-watt smile, the first real one he'd seen since before Vanessa died.

It lit up Sarah's face, chasing away the exhaustion and sadness and fear. Made her look younger—and more beautiful. That same spark of awareness sizzled inside of him.

He tried to look anywhere but at the woman sitting across the table from him, yet his gaze was drawn to her like a magnet. Despite the fact that she was rumpled and her clothes were covered with ketchup stains, she was beautiful. The way she held the baby and interacted with her children, the joy she took from being with her family, was the most attractive thing he'd ever seen.

He wanted her, needed her. That she wasn't perfect, that she was vulnerable and subject to fits of temper only made her more interesting to him. More desirable.

God, he really was a sick bastard—and a selfish one. Though he felt guilty as hell about it, desire settled in his chest and breathing became increasingly uncomfortable.

"Let it go, Reece," she said, her voice soft and warm as she continued their conversation. "I'm going to."

"Just like that?"

"Just like that," she confirmed. "I've never been good at holding a grudge."

He searched her open, honest expression for some hint that she was holding out on him. But Sarah was guileless and more forgiving than he deserved.

God knows, Vanessa had never been so easygoing. Where Sarah was quick to release her anger, Vanessa had been able to keep her mad up for days, even weeks. No matter how bad he felt over some real, or imagined, transgression, she always found a way to make him feel worse. Had always found a way to draw it out until he'd brought her the right amount of flowers and small gifts and apologies to soothe her ruffled feathers.

It was refreshing not to have to play that game with Sarah. To know that she meant what she said and punishment was the furthest thing from her mind. Suddenly, he realized that he didn't want to bury the attraction. Didn't want to let it go.

Sarah was beautiful—inside and out. Her too-prominent cheekbones and the shadows under her eyes made her look more delicate, more vulnerable, more in need of care. He could spend hours staring at her, learning every nuance of her face.

But if he did act on the attraction, if he did give in to it—he'd be out on his ass faster than he could apologize. There was no way Sarah would put up with that, not from any man let alone her best friend's husband.

The baby whimpered and Sarah immediately focused her attention on Rose. He felt the loss of her attention keenly.

"Do you want me to hold her?" he asked. "So that you have a chance to eat?" He nodded at her untouched hamburger and fries.

"That's okay. I can eat later."

"Don't be ridiculous." He reached for Rose.

Sarah relinquished Rose with a reluctance that surprised him. She'd been on her own for so long that he would have expected her to be thrilled at the chance to offload for a while. Yet she seemed almost lost.

"Hey, are you okay?" he asked quietly.

"Yeah, I'm fine." This time her smile was obviously forced, more of a grimace.

"I—" Rose fussed against him and panic ripped through his heart. "Am I hurting her?" He quickly adjusted her in his arms. What had he been thinking, volunteering to take the baby? He knew nothing about babies and now he'd hurt her—

"Here." He tried to thrust Rose at Sarah. "You take her back."

But Sarah merely shook her head and busied herself eating her hamburger. "You've got to figure this out sometime."

"But she's not happy." Cold sweat poured down his back. "I think she's going to—" Rose's long, unhappy wail stopped him. He looked at Sarah pleadingly, but she continued to eat while their daughter worked herself into a full-blown fit.

Gritting his teeth, Reece bounced the baby a little bit, as he murmured nonsense to her. "It's okay, little Rosie-posie. Daddy's got you, Daddy's got you."

Unfortunately, the fact that he had her seemed to be part of the problem. Rosie merely screwed up her little face and screamed louder. "Sarah, what do I do?"

"Try burping her." She popped a fry in her mouth. "You took her before I'd finished and the change in position might be hurting her tummy."

Gingerly, more gingerly than he'd even thought

possible, Reece shifted the baby onto his shoulder then began patting her like Sarah had taught him. Within a couple seconds the crying stopped and soon after a delicate burp emerged.

He nearly sagged in relief.

"Nice job," Sarah said as she winked at him. "You did it."

"I did, didn't I?" Even he could hear the pride in his voice. He'd finally done something right.

"Yep." She gathered the trash on the table. "Now I think I should go round up the boys so we can go home. All three of them need baths tonight."

"Don't leave me." Was she insane? What if Rose started crying again?

"You'll do fine, Reece," Sarah said with a shake of her head. "Just keep her in that position and talk to her a little." She wandered to the far side of the playscape to find the boys.

Okay. So he would have to cope, no matter how frightening this little person was with her cries and whimpers and little sighs.

Just then Rose chose to sigh, squirming against him until her face was buried in his neck. For a moment everything was perfect. The baby was content, happy even, and he felt a peace unlike anything he'd ever experienced.

He had a moment of clarity. This was what Vanessa had searched for, what she'd craved. She'd done every-thing to have a child—taken shots, consulted infertility doctor after infertility doctor, taken her temperature, given up favorite foods. And throughout the entire process he'd tried to be supportive, but he hadn't been sure he'd wanted a baby. Hadn't known what kind of father he would be. Between the beer and the beatings, his old man had been a regular what-not-to-do parenting manual.

But now Reece got what had driven Vanessa, what joy she'd been seeking. It seemed unfair that he was the one sitting here enjoying Rose, reveling in the feel of her soft body pressed against his own. It should have been Vanessa. The guilt—at holding Rose now, at wanting Sarah, at not trying harder to understand Vanessa—colored the moment and threatened to overwhelm him. Regardless of what she'd done to him, Reece had let his wife down.

Rose cuddled into his chest, the movement reminding him he had a second chance here and now. He almost didn't recognize the contentment he felt.

But could she breathe with her nose pressed up against his throat like that? He held his breath for a few seconds, his hand resting on her back as he waited for her exhale. Nothing happened. He panicked. Ripping Rose off his shoulder as his very rusty infant CPR knowledge flooded his head, he yelled for Sarah, ignoring the looks of annoyance other diners shot him.

To Sarah's credit, she came running, arriving as Rose lifted a little fist and smacked him in the mouth.

Relief swamped him. There would be time to be embarrassed later.

Because God knew, this parenting thing was a lot harder than he had originally anticipated.

CHAPTER SIX

AFTER THREE DAYS of attempting to keep up with Sarah, Reece was exhausted. It was the middle of the night and he should be sound asleep. Instead, he lay in an unfamiliar bed, staring at an unfamiliar ceiling.

How did Sarah do it all, day after day? Already he wanted to throw in the towel and beg for mercy. She got up at four-thirty, when Rose cried for a bottle. After feeding the baby and setting her in the swing, Sarah would work until the boys woke.

At that point, she would feed and dress the kids before dropping Justin and Johnny at school then coming home to start on the never-ending chores—laundry, doing dishes, scrubbing bathrooms, tidying the cars and action figures and trains that littered every space. Among those tasks, Sarah put in time on her clients' projects, cared for Rose and cooked, before picking up the boys from school. The evenings were a frenzy of eating, bathing and playing until the boys went to bed and Sarah spent another couple of hours on her business.

The routine was a delicate balance that depended on Sarah working eighteen or nineteen hours straight, then going to bed for two or three hours before the baby woke and the cycle started again. He didn't know how she did it. Didn't want to know, to tell the truth.

All he really wanted to know was how to fix it.

But he didn't have a clue where to start.

Was a housekeeper the answer? A nanny? He'd hire one or the other—or both—if he thought Sarah would let him get away with it. He had the money for it, but Sarah was stubborn about things like this. After Mike left, he remembered Vanessa trying to convince Sarah to hire some help around the house. She'd said she liked to do things herself and she didn't want some stranger taking care of her children.

But surely a cleaning person once or twice a week wouldn't upset Sarah's sense of independence. He'd broach the subject tomorrow.

He was drifting, halfway between sleep and wakefulness, when he heard Rose crying. Part of him wanted to roll over and ignore the sound—Sarah was good at getting the baby quickly—but guilt prodded him. Hadn't he just decided that Sarah needed help?

The crying wasn't stopping. In fact, it was getting louder. He sprang out of bed, reaching for the unfamiliar pajama bottoms he now kept close. He all but ran to the nursery. Something must be very wrong.

Rose was enraged. Her legs were tangled in the light blanket Sarah always covered her with and her fists flailed furiously as she struggled to roll onto her tummy.

He crossed the room, bent over the crib and picked

up the angry baby. Tucking her against his chest, like Sarah had taught him, he closed his eyes in sheer relief as she gave one shuddering breath then buried her face against his neck.

He stood, cuddling Rose for long moments. Letting her sweet baby scent calm his thundering heart and panicked mind. Savoring the feel of her in his arms.

Eventually she began to squirm against him, little mewls escaping her perfect rosebud lips. She was hungry.

He would have to feed her.

Even while he wrestled with his doubts about this task and a part of him wondered where Sarah was—she never ignored the baby—he crept down the stairs with Rosie still cradled against his chest. Sarah always made a bottle before going to bed and stored it in the refrigerator. Surely he could manage to heat it up without any major catastrophes.

Getting the bottle from the fridge without dropping the baby proved trickier than he thought. But he got it uncapped and into the microwave. As he set the appliance at the correct power and time, he experienced a sense of relief, and triumph. Maybe not rocket science, but he accomplished it.

While the bottle heated up, he changed Rosie's diaper. It wasn't the prettiest—or quickest—diaper change on record, but he was inordinately pleased with his effort.

He was doing this. He was taking care of his daughter, by himself. For a man who designed signature buildings all over the world, the realization was humbling.

And he wasn't finished. Rose was starting to whimper and the microwave had dinged a few minutes before.

"Yeah," he muttered. "You're really getting this fatherhood thing down."

He settled into the rocking chair in Rosie's room to feed her. There was something soothing in the ritual, something calming for him as well as the baby. Even as he worried about her choking on the milk and obsessed about getting her to burp, it felt right.

As he laid Rose in her crib, he thought about Vanessa. She should have been here. It should have been her rocking and soothing the baby. Bathing her. Feeding her. Loving her.

And that's how it would have been. Vanessa would have cared for Rose exclusively while he continued to pour himself into his work. There would have been few shared moments and little sense they were in this parenting thing together.

The way he was already feeling with Sarah.

The thought felt wrong, disloyal, even though it was true. He did feel close to Sarah, as though they had a special connection. One he'd rarely experienced with his wife no matter how much he'd loved her.

He froze as he realized he hadn't thought of Vanessa all day until now. How could that be? It had only been seven months. Seven months since he'd held his wife. Kissed her. Made love to her. He couldn't be forgetting about her. Couldn't be thinking about Sarah—with her stunning eyes and generous spirit—far too often.

Yet he was.

What kind of husband did that make him? He'd never fully supported Vanessa's longing for a child—to the point a rift developed in their relationship—yet here he was embracing not only that child, but also her mother as if he'd never wanted to be anywhere else.

He owed Vanessa so much and had no way to make amends. The guilt assailed him. What the hell was he supposed to do?

SARAH STARED AT REECE hovering over the baby's crib, her heart thundering in her chest.

He had taken care of the baby?

By himself?

Without her?

The pain pierced. She was no longer solely responsible for her little girl's life. Rose's father also had the ability to take care of her, to soothe her hurts and rock her to sleep. It was a powerful realization, one that nearly crippled Sarah.

She'd been on her own for too long—taking care of the boys, then doing the same for Rose. Taking care of Tad and her mother after her dad had left. Even taking care of Vanessa, when things got too much for her to handle. How daunting then for Sarah to admit she had someone to lean on. Someone to take the burden from her when it got too heavy—at least for as long as Reece hung around. That he was willing to take care of her, if she let him.

Maybe it was because of those thoughts that she noticed, for the first time, the play of light and shadows over Reece's bare chest as he shifted. His very attractive, very well-muscled chest.

Maybe it was because she was looking at him as the father of *her* child. Not as Vanessa's husband.

Whatever the reason was—shock, grief or simple biology—Sarah gasped as her nipples hardened. As her body responded once again to the nearness and warmth of this man.

Reece turned at her gasp, gave her a little smile that had her stomach tightening.

What was wrong with her? This was Vanessa's husband. How could Sarah possibly, even for a second, have noticed—

"I didn't want to wake you." His words invaded her self-flagellation. "You've been so tired."

"Thanks." She cleared her throat, sought to control the unruly reaction of her body. "Did you feed her?" she whispered, walking closer to look at her perfect little girl.

"I did. And I changed her diaper."

He sounded so proud. And, lord, what that domestic prowess did to the hormones rocketing through her. Hormones that reminded her how long it had been since she'd been this close to a half-naked man.

But for how long would he stay interested in playing house, the cynical little voice inside of her asked. He was helpful now, but what happened when Rose got sick, as babies did? What happened when he found a woman—one who didn't want a baby that wasn't her own? What happened when work—and life—interfered?

Rose and the boys and Sarah would come in last. Just like always.

Thankfully, her macabre thoughts killed the sparks of desire. Her body might not understand all the reasons Reece was so incredibly bad for her, but her mind certainly did. And at the moment, her mind was firmly in control.

"I appreciate your help." Her voice was stilted, cold and she could see that the difference registered on Reece as she backed away from the crib. From him.

"No problem." He kept his voice low, nearly toneless, but his eyes were filled with questions—questions she had no desire to answer. Questions she wasn't even sure she *could* answer.

Retreating from the room as quickly and soundlessly as she could, Sarah headed for the safety of her room. But Reece was right behind her and he caught her elbow to stop her flight.

"Are you okay?"

"It's the middle of the night, Reece. I'm not really at my best right now."

"That's not what I meant and you know it." His grip tightened, not to the point of pain, but definitely enough for her to know that he meant business.

The dominance of the gesture set her teeth on edge, especially as he had no right to it. This was *her* house. These were *her* children and *her* problems.

He was the interloper with his too-masculine chest and too-pretty face. He was the one making her hormones jump around like frogs on speed. And he was the one who had come into this equation seven months too late.

Sarah was shocked at the vehemence of her thoughts. She had been so sure she was over this.

So where was the resistance coming from? Where had this anger been lurking?

She didn't want to be like this, didn't want to be so angry. She had always rolled with the punches. Even when Mike left her, six months pregnant, she hadn't been this bitter. This furious.

So why now? Why with Reece, who had done nothing but try to help her?

Even as she told herself to calm down, to let go of the irrational burden, she felt her fury ratchet higher.

"You're going to want to let go of me, Reece." She spoke through her teeth as she tried to yank her elbow from his grip.

He watched her for long seconds before his fingers slowly uncurled. "I'm sorry. I don't know why I did that."

To his credit, he did look bewildered. As if this sudden shift in their relationship—from cordial friends to something deeper, darker—was as surprising to him as it was to her.

Once again her stomach flipped, and once again she ignored it, refusing to acknowledge anything.

"Don't do it again." She shot him a look that said she meant business—it was the same look she'd used on Mike when he'd overstepped his boundaries with her. Then, knowing nothing good could happen if she remained in such proximity to Reece, she shut herself behind the relative safety of her bedroom door.

CHAPTER SEVEN

TWO MONTHS LATER, Sarah was feeding Rose her breakfast when she heard the front door open. "Honey, I'm
home," Reece called in the cheesy sit-com voice he
used when he was trying to make her laugh. It usually
worked and today was no exception.

"Did the boys get into their classroom okay?" she
asked as his footsteps sounded behind her.

"They did." He stopped to give Rose a kiss on her
fuzzy baby hair before heading to the refrigerator.
"What do you want to eat?"

"Whatever you're having."

She glanced behind her in time to see him pull out a
gallon of milk and some strawberries before heading
into the pantry. "Did you give the teacher the check for
their hot lunch?"

"I did," he said, pulling two bowls from a cabinet.
"And she said Justin and Johnny are doing very well."

"Really?" Sarah's heart jumped as she turned to him.
"You asked her?"

"I didn't have to. She volunteered the information."

"Really? So do you think she meant it?"

"Of course she meant it. The boys are taking to school like champs—even I can tell that. Stop worrying."

"Easy for you to say." She wiped a damp cloth over her oatmeal-and-applesauce-covered daughter. "You're not the one who had to go to the principal's office when they clogged up the school toilet with cars for the third time."

"Touché." He handed her a bowl of cereal then took a seat across the table from her and Rose. "But I am the one who has learned how to take care of the toilet here so that half our monthly income doesn't go to Vince the plumber."

"There is that."

"There is indeed. And—" he gestured with his cereal bowl "—I make a mean breakfast."

"Yes, you do."

"So, perhaps I'm worth keeping around for a while."

"Perhaps." His words echoed in Sarah's head as she ate her cereal. Reece really had made a difference around the house since he'd moved in. He'd stuck to his word about making things easier for her. He took the boys to school each morning so that she could spend some time with Rose. He played with the boys after she picked them up from school and had turned into quite the drill sergeant when it came to getting Justin and Johnny to tidy up their toys.

Not to mention the most startling fact of all—that he had become a natural with Rose. He bathed her, diapered her, fed her—in essence all the things that Sarah herself did. And he never complained, even when he took his turn doing the night shifts.

All in all, things were working out much better than she ever could have imagined. Of course, the house-keeper Reece had hired to come in twice a week to clean and do laundry helped. At first she'd wanted to fight him about Eva—and had certainly wanted to cover the costs herself—but Reece had been adamant. He would take care of it.

That seemed to be his mantra and one he lived up to with incredible accuracy. So what did it say about her that she constantly waited for the other shoe to drop? Constantly waited for him to have enough of the trials and tribulations that came from looking after a family that wasn't his own and walk out.

Except he never made her feel as though they weren't family, never told her that the boys weren't his respon-sibility. He'd even cut out a lot of his work travel so that he could be with them. If she wasn't careful, she was going to start believing they were a family.

Instinctively her mind shied away from the thought. They weren't. Reece wasn't her husband. He was Vanessa's husband. And that was more than fine with Sarah. After Mike, she certainly wasn't in the market for another husband anyway.

Except sometimes, when she wasn't prepared, Reece would smile at her and her heart would beat a little too hard. Her pulse would race a little too fast and her body would respond before she could remind herself that he was off-limits.

"Hey, Sarah, where'd you go?"

Reece's voice jerked her out of her thoughts. "I don't

know. Just imagining what other terrors the boys had in store for us this year." She was uncomfortable with the lie, but she wasn't about to tell him the truth.

"You worry too much. They're just normal boys. High-strung, sure, but good-hearted. They don't mean to get into trouble. It's just that they're—"

"Curious. I know. At the rate they're going one—or both—of them won't make it to adolescence."

"You'd be surprised. Kids are more resilient than you think."

"I know you're right."

"But moms worry." He reached out and ruffled her hair, much as he did to the boys. It was a gesture of careless affection and absolutely not meant to inspire the jump in her heart rate. "I remember Vanessa used to say—"

He cut off in midsentence.

"What did she say?"

"Nothing. Just that she didn't know how you and some of her other friends did it. How you learned to balance the worry and the need to wrap your children in cotton with their need to explore and learn and make mistakes."

"I think it's the hardest thing about being a parent." She slipped Rose out of her high chair and handed her to Reece before crossing to the sink to put their breakfast dishes in the dishwasher.

"I don't know how I'm going to learn that," he said as he lifted Rose in the air and blew on her tummy. The baby laughed, kicked her feet, grabbing onto her daddy's hair to show her approval.

"You'll do fine."

He glanced at her. "Do you really think so?"

"I know so. You're doing an incredible job with her. And when it comes time for her to take her first steps, you'll let her do that—even knowing she's going to fall down and get hurt more than once."

"Don't be too sure about that." Reece gave a shudder. "I might force her to wear a helmet and knee pads before I let her loose."

Sarah laughed. "You wouldn't be the first father to do that."

"Probably not." Reece played with Rose for a few minutes as she got the dishwasher on then started a load of laundry. Of everything he'd done for her this touched her the most—the time he took to play with his daughter.

"Well, I've got to get to work." Reece handed Rose to Sarah reluctantly, his hands lingering on the baby's cheeks before he finally managed to tear himself away. "I've got clients coming in from the West Coast to look at my new design."

"For the Westmont building?" she asked, as she balanced Rose on a hip.

"Yeah."

"How did that turn out? I know you were having some trouble with it."

"I got everything worked out with Matt's help. It's all good." He grabbed his briefcase and headed for the door. "I'll be home in plenty of time for you to get to the open house at the boys' school."

"Geez, I forgot all about it."

"I figured you had, since you hadn't mentioned it. That's what I'm here for." With a wink, he was out the door.

How could she have been so careless, as to have forgotten the meeting with the boys' teacher.

But as she settled Rose on her office floor with a bunch of toys, she wondered what had her so upset. That she'd forgotten the open house? Or that Reece had been around to remind her?

It was the latter, she decided nearly an hour later as she struggled with a Web design. She was coming to depend on Reece more and more, even though she knew she couldn't. That's what had screwed up her mother so much when her father left—her utter dependence on him to meet both her material and emotional needs.

Sarah wouldn't make the same mistake. So what if Reece remembered open house? It didn't mean anything. And she would be just fine when he left.

Satisfied with her reasoning, she finally gave the computer her full attention. And did her damnedest to ignore the hollowness that had taken up residence in the center of her chest.

REECE WAS SITTING on the floor in the family room, Rose next to him as he played trucks with Johnny and Justin. The boys were so cute, and so sweet, it was hard to get mad at them. Even when they'd scribbled with permanent marker all over his light table he couldn't keep his mad up. How could he when they hung their heads pitifully and explained how exciting it had been to see the light shine through the fantastic designs made by the marker?

Sarah had nearly died, had insisted on replacing the table for him despite his objections. The one she got him was bigger and better than the model he kept at home— was comparable to the ones he had at the office. He'd told her it was too much, but she hadn't listened.

"Look out, Uncle Reece, here I come," Johnny shouted as his 18-wheeler barreled down on Reece's dump truck.

"I'm going to get there first," Justin called, pointing his gigantic fire truck at him.

"Hey," said Reece, engaging in more evasive maneuvers than he'd ever had to do in driver's ed. "What did my dump truck ever do to you?"

"You're not a real dump truck!" Justin shouted happily, the gleam of battle in his eyes.

"I'm not?" He stared at the red, yellow and blue truck in confusion. "Then what am I?"

"You're a robber. You just stole a gazillion dollars and you've hidden it in the back of the truck. You're trying to get away," Johnny exclaimed, as he moved his truck neatly in front of Reece's.

"Yeah. But we're not gonna let you, 'cuz we're the good guys." Justin crashed into his truck from behind, sending it spinning across the carpet.

"You don't really think I'm going to give up so easily, do you?" Reece gave the most evil laugh he was capable of as he spun his truck around and plowed it directly into Johnny's rig.

The boys shrieked and Rose giggled. The sound had

echoes of Sarah's laugh, surprising Reece. She seemed more like her old self these days, more like the woman who took on the world her way. Early on he'd learned to get out of her way when she was on a roll, otherwise he'd end up a pancake in the middle of the road.

Life with her was exciting, intriguing. More than once he'd found himself with the urge to kiss her, which was more than a little disconcerting.

Not to mention, frightening. With Sarah's independent streak, she'd probably solve the problem by punching him in the nose then kicking him out of her house.

She was totally different than Van had been. Van had always consulted him about a decision before she made it—no matter how small or inconsequential. She'd asked his advice on everything and had listened to it almost exclusively.

With Sarah, half the time she seemed to forget he was around. Just last week he'd found her under the sink, fixing the garbage disposal. When he'd demanded to know why she hadn't called him, she'd looked at him like he'd lost his mind, and told him that she didn't need his help.

More and more he saw that that was true. No matter how much he disliked admitting it, Sarah didn't need him—and probably never would. Sure, she'd been floundering when he'd first arrived, but not so much now. He was becoming superfluous. As if he was nothing more than someone else Sarah had to take care of—in short, a failure. For a man who had spent his life avoiding that feeling, it was more than a little uncomfortable.

"Do it again, Uncle Reece! Do it again!"

Johnny's voice pulled his attention back to the game of dodge and crash. "You bet, guys." Stretching out on his stomach, he plowed his truck into Justin's this time and grinned as the boys giggled.

Rosie watched with rapt interest, so he did it again and again until he heard the click of heels behind him. Turning, he nearly swallowed his tongue at the sight of Sarah. Most of the blood in his head made a rapid trip south.

Gone was the work-at-home mom he was accustomed to. In her place was a blond bombshell—slender but with curves in all the right places. And legs that seemed to go on for miles.

"Is that a new dress?" he asked, his voice much hoarser than usual.

She glanced down as her hand swept over the skirt. "It is. I found it at the mall last week, when I was picking up shoes for Rose."

"You look good."

"Really?" Her smile was tentative.

"Yeah." Oh yeah. Good enough to have his libido leaping to life.

She was Van's friend, he reminded himself viciously. His wife's friend. Enough plotting schemes to get her horizontal.

But she was also the mother of his child, a little voice whispered insidiously. That had to count for something. And they'd been living together for months.

But not in the conventional sense, he reminded himself, squeezing his hands into fists in an effort to fight the arousal. And she would be shocked—horrified—if she had any idea what he was thinking.

Hell, he was horrified himself—even as he couldn't get the idea of touching her out of his traitorous brain. He knew from experience that her skin was almost as soft as Rose's and so much more fragrant. But tonight, it was glowing, luminescent. Beautiful. The dress—the same indigo color as her eyes—made everything about her a little softer than it had been before.

"Well—" she glanced at her watch "—I've got to get going or I'll be late."

"I've got things under control here."

"Okay." She hesitated, as if she didn't know what to say.

"I've got it," he reiterated, his voice made harsher than he'd intended by the sexual awareness still zipping around inside of him.

She stiffened at his tone, her eyes going from pleased to wary in the space of a heartbeat. "I've got dinner in the oven. It's just a casserole, but there's fresh bread next to the stove and a salad in the fridge. I shouldn't be late."

She turned, and before he could think of something to say to make up for his churlish behavior, she was gone—leaving a cloud of sexy-as-hell perfume in her wake.

CHAPTER EIGHT

SARAH SHIFTED in the kindergarten chair, uncomfortable despite herself. It wasn't the size of the chair that brought her such discomfort, however, but the look in Reece's eyes. The look that said she was hot.

That he wanted her.

That she turned him on.

It had been so long since she'd seen that look on a man's face. And Reece had had it in spades, though she'd tried—numerous times—to tell herself she was mistaken.

"Mrs. Martin, it's so good to see you." The boys' teacher approached with a big smile.

Scrambling to her feet, Sarah tried to work up a smile of her own, despite the butterflies doing the samba in her stomach. "Hello, Mrs. De Salvo. How are you?"

"I'm doing very well. And so are your boys."

"Really?"

"Absolutely. They're a little high-spirited—" the teacher's eyes twinkled "—but they're very sweet. Always interested in what I'm teaching, always volunteering to do whatever chore needs to be done."

"I'm glad to hear that. With everything that's happened, I've worried."

"Well, don't. They're the youngest in the class, and there are always more adjustment issues for the young ones. No reason for you to be concerned—"

Concerned was an understatement. After her second visit to the principal's office in three weeks, Sarah had decided that she was a failure as a mother. But Reece had merely laughed, pointing out that the boys never did anything malicious. They simply wanted to see how things worked.

But then Reece was good at calming her down. He always seemed to have a handle on what was going on around him, around them. Even this sexual attraction between them didn't seem to startle him—

"Does that sound okay? Mrs. Martin?"

Mortified, Sarah jerked her attention back to Justin and Johnny's teacher. The woman had obviously asked her a question and she'd been too caught up in thoughts of Reece to answer. Her cheeks burned, and she felt like her thoughts were written across her forehead.

"I'm sorry. Could you repeat the question?"

Mrs. De Salvo gave her a strange look, then said, "I was asking if you could donate a few items to the treasure box." She gestured to the large chest in the corner of the room that Justin and Johnny had only recently behaved well enough to get treats from. "We're running low."

"Um, sure. Of course." Sarah forced a smile. "I'll stop by the store tomorrow."

"Excellent." The teacher beamed at her. "Please, stay and look around at all the work the boys have been doing."

"I will, thank you."

But as Sarah wandered the room, pretending to study childishly scrawled stories and pictures, she obsessed over the heat that had literally poured off Reece earlier. A mirroring heat simmered in her own system.

She stooped to look at pictures of a science experiment the students had done. But even as she searched for Justin's and Johnny's smiling faces, all she could think was that she should have known better. They were two healthy adults living in the same house, taking care of their children—and each other. Neither one of them had had sex in quite a while.

Maybe that's why she'd noticed him before—nothing this overt of course, but the awareness had been building. The proximity, the opportunity, the abstinence— it was the perfect recipe for desire. That was it. This tension wasn't really about her and Reece as people but about the situation.

The intensity of Reece's stare flashed through her mind.

Yeah. Right. The situational explanation was pretty and neat but it just didn't cut it. She wanted Reece and only him. And, judging by that look he'd given her, he wanted her as much.

What a mess. That wall she'd put up between her and Reece—the wall that marked him as Vanessa's husband— was crumbling. And despite the guilt, Sarah wanted the barrier gone. Some friend she was to lust after Reece.

She dreaded going home, dreaded facing him with her body so alive it was painful, dreaded dealing with that same body's shameful betrayal.

Two other parents came up behind her and she moved to the next board, where the students had drawn pictures of their recent trip to the zoo. As she studied Johnny's version of a snarling tiger, she couldn't help feeling as if there was a scarlet *A* across her chest, visible for everyone to see.

Van might be dead, but Reece was still her husband. Would always be her husband—and Sarah would never be anything but an interloper. One more reason that she had to get her emotions under control.

Besides, in purely selfish terms, she had no desire to be the rebound woman. How could any woman compete with the memory of a wife?

"The pictures are great, aren't they?"

"I'm sorry?" She turned to the extremely attractive man standing next to her. Blond with deep green eyes that crinkled at the corners, he had a smile that instantly made her respond in kind.

"The pictures." He tapped his finger on what she thought might be an elephant. "My daughter, Brittani, has a thing for hippopotami."

Or a hippopotamus. "She's very good." Then she pointed out her boys' pictures.

"Wow, twins, huh?"

"Indeed."

"That must be a lot to handle for a—" he glanced at her left hand "—single mom."

Alarms went off in her head as she clued in that the warmth in his eyes—the warmth she assumed was for his daughter's picture—was actually for her.

"Um, yeah, but—" Her brain seemed unable to formulate even the most basic answer. How long had it been since a man had hit on her? Too long, if her only response was to blush and stammer.

Thankfully, he seemed to understand her predicament and was gentleman enough not to push. Instead, he winked and said, "It was nice meeting you."

"Uh, yes. You, too." Sarah watched him walk away with a nearly overwhelming feeling of relief. Obviously, she still wasn't ready for anything to happen between her and a man.

So she would bury this whole sexual attraction thing with Reece. If she ignored it, surely it would go away.

Mollified Sarah drove home and tried her best to ignore the fact that she was lying to herself.

REECE'S HEART POUNDED a little faster as he heard the garage door open. The kids were all asleep and he'd hoped to have a few minutes to chill. A few minutes to tackle the reaction he'd had to Sarah earlier. But she was back earlier than expected.

"Hey." Sarah's voice was strangely subdued as she laid her purse on the kitchen counter and smiled at him.

"Hey, yourself." Damn, she looked as beautiful and enticing as she had before she'd left earlier in the evening. Leashing his libido, he asked, "How was back-to-school night?"

"It was good. Mrs. De Salvo seems like she'll be great for them. I like her discipline rules and what she's planning this semester."

"I'm glad." He nodded toward the bottle of wine on the coffee table. "Grab a glass."

To his surprise, she did. He could count on one finger the number of times he'd seen Sarah drink since he'd moved in. But he didn't comment, merely poured the merlot into her glass.

"To what do I owe this honor?"

"I don't know—I was tense." He shrugged. "Needed to unwind, I guess."

"Did things go okay with your clients this morning?" She leaned forward, concerned, and he caught the sweet and spicy scent of her. She smelled like the magnolias in his backyard—tempting and oh-so-beautiful. Combined with lingering notes of cinnamon from the snickerdoodles she'd baked the boys earlier, she was almost irresistible.

"It went fine." He tried to breathe through his mouth to end the torment. "They wrote me a big, fat check and are ready to get started as soon as Matt and I can pull everything together."

"That's fabulous. I know how hard you've worked on that proposal."

It was great news—for his career and for the company he and Matt had started eight years before with little more than AutoCAD and a drafting table. But at the moment he was more interested in watching the light play over the red and gold streaks in Sarah's hair than he was in talking about the client he had all but bled for.

"Yeah. I guess."

"What's wrong?" She put a hand over his and he nearly jumped out of his skin. Nearly jumped her.

"There will be a lot of travel—at least in the first few months. Matt can take care of some, but—" Sarah licked her lips and he struggled not to groan. His overheated brain couldn't help imagining what it would be like to have that pink tongue of hers over—

He slammed door after door against the need rocketing through him. What was wrong with him? He never let himself think of Sarah like this. Always stopped his mind from wandering down a path that might take him here. Yet from the moment he'd seen her earlier tonight, he had been almost consumed by thoughts of her. Desperate for the chance to hold her, to kiss her. To sate the rip-roaring hunger inside of him.

"That's okay. We'll manage. And you know, if there's anything you need help with, you only have to ask."

Oh yeah, he had something he wanted her help with. But if he told her exactly what he needed, she'd probably run screaming for her room. Or the nearest weapon.

"It'll all work out," he agreed in a voice that he knew was way too tense.

Out of the corner of his eye, he caught the tensing of her body, caught the angling of her hips and shoulders toward him, even as she maintained a more than appropriate distance. Was she somehow feeling the same way? Was she having the same cravings for him that he was for her?

Lust slammed through him at the thought, eating him

from the inside out. Suddenly, it took every ounce of self-control he had not to wrap his hands around her arms and close the short distance. He wanted her in his lap, her hips moving restlessly against his. He wanted her mouth on his, her tongue tangled temptingly with his. He wanted her breasts in his hand, her nipples peaked against fingers that ached with the need to touch her. To be inside her.

He tried to stop himself, tried to move away. But the air was moving through his lungs like a bellows, sexual attraction sharp and inescapable between them.

"Reece." Sarah's voice was shaky, her eyes pleading. The hand she held out to him anything but steady. He didn't know if it was an invitation or a plea for him to stop. He didn't care. He was too far gone, his hunger for her a raging beast he had no hope of controlling.

Grasping her hands, he gave a sharp tug and quickly had her exactly where he wanted her. Next to him, on top of him, surrounded by him. Their faces so close that they breathed the same air, their bodies pressed so tightly together that he could feel the frantic pulse of her heart against his chest. Knew that she could feel the crazy pounding of his, as well.

Part of him wanted to take her mouth quickly, to devour her in a series of fast, sharp bites. Another part wanted to savor, to bask in the feel of a soft, sensual woman in his arms again. And not just any woman, but Sarah. So kind, so loving, so beautiful.

With one movement she took the choice away from

him. Leaning in, she brushed her lips against his and set off an explosion he had no hopes of controlling.

With a low groan, he shifted his hands, sinking his fingers into the short satin of her hair. Chaining her to him as he tilted his head and prepared to take what she had so sweetly offered him.

Panic and need and desire churned in Sarah's stomach as Reece's hands knotted in her hair. She wanted him, wanted this. Needed this with a desperation she'd never imagined possible. All her misgivings danced in the back of her head, all the reasons she'd given herself earlier about why this was a bad idea. But as his mouth hovered above hers, she couldn't bring herself to care.

Later was time enough for the recriminations.

With her breath catching in her throat, Sarah let her eyes flutter closed. She savored the heat of his breath against her cheeks, her lips. Relished the hardness of his body where it pushed against her own. Waited for the feel of his mouth over hers.

And waited.

And waited.

Confused, embarrassed, wondering if she'd misread the signals, she opened her eyes and was snared instantly by his gaze. Only then, when they were connected—eye to eye—did Reece's lips settle over her own.

He robbed her of air with the first touch of his mouth. With the second touch, he gave her his breath and with the third, took inside of him everything she had to give.

Just that easily she was lost.

Just that easily she was his.

Reece teased her, played with her—his lips soft and gentle and coaxing—until she moaned and melted against him. Until she opened to him.

Then his tongue swept inside, toying with her, tasting her, and Sarah met him stroke for stroke, letting her tongue tangle sweetly with his.

Following his example, she tasted him, too. Caught his lower lip between her teeth and sucked until he groaned, his hands tightening where they were buried in her curls. He tasted delicious—exotic. Salty like the ocean. Fresh like the rain. Tart like the lemonade that was her favorite treat.

His mouth hardened at her uninhibited response, took command, devoured her, until all she could think of was him. Until all she could want was him. She was sinking, drowning, awash in layers of sensation she'd never before imagined.

He pulled back a little and she whimpered, lifting her own arms to wrap around his neck and hold him in place. Hold him to her. She knew she should let him stop, but she didn't want to let him go. Couldn't let him go, if she was being honest. The need was growing in her, making her body pulse, making her ache like she hadn't ached in six long years. Longer. Maybe forever. The thought had her heart beating too fast and her lungs burning for air. Tightening her arms around him, she pressed herself more fully against him and gave herself up to him. Totally. Completely.

His mouth grew more urgent, his kisses deeper and

darker and oh, so devastating. He pulled back slowly this time, kissing the corners of her mouth. Sweet licks that had heat shimmying through her. Soft nibbles that had her body straining to be closer to him. Sharp nips that both enticed and commanded.

And when he ran his tongue over her top lip then under it, she nearly imploded. The warmth that had already seeped into her very pores erupted, shot flames into every part of her.

She moaned low in her throat, and just that easily his kiss went from gentle to rough. Exciting. Devastating. He shifted, pushing her down until she was prone on the sofa and his body covered hers. His hard, sexy heavily muscled body.

As he settled between her thighs, his erection pressed against her and she arched into the delicious pressure. It was her turn to bite at him, to suck his tongue into her mouth. His answering thrusts told her how much he'd enjoyed her uncharacteristic boldness.

Breathless, she tilted her head to offer him her jaw, her throat. To offer him everything, though she knew that she wasn't ready. That he wasn't ready. That they weren't ready. But at this moment, with his body against hers, with her body tense and tormented, it didn't matter. Nothing mattered except—

"Shit." Reece ripped his mouth from hers, then lay panting—his face buried in the couch cushion—for long seconds. She wanted to howl, to weep, to beg him to continue before her long-dormant body spontaneously combusted.

"What's wrong?" she gasped, her hands running frantically down his back. "Reece, why—"

"The baby." It was a groan—low, harsh and nearly unrecognizable. At first she didn't understand. Then she heard Rose's cries turning into high-pitched wails.

"I've got her." Reece sat up slowly, and it was all she could do to keep her eyes from his obvious arousal.

"No." She slipped out of his arms before he could protest. Or she could forget about her baby, crying. "It's my turn. You put her down."

"But—"

She shot him a smile as she took one trembling step toward the stairs, not sure her shaky legs would actually support her. But her knees locked and she managed to stay upright. "I'll be back in a few minutes. Okay?"

He nodded, his face solemn, his eyes black with desire. "I'll be here."

It took longer than a few minutes to comfort Rose and get her back to sleep. It was too early for another bottle and the baby didn't seem hungry so much as in need of some cuddling from her mother.

As she rocked, she thought of Rose and Reece, Johnny and Justin. And Vanessa. Sarah thought of her friend most of all. She could still feel Reece's lips on her own, knew if she were to look in a mirror her mouth would be swollen from his kisses. She wanted him still, needed him with an intensity that bordered on madness. Even as she sat here in the dark holding his child, her child—Vanessa's child—her body burned for his.

How could she have done this, how could she be doing it still? This was Reece. Reece.

Vanessa's husband.

Rose's father.

Sarah's friend.

How could she want him when everything she believed marked him as off-limits? How could she hunger for him when she knew that the last woman he'd made love to had been her best friend?

Sarah shuddered at the thought, her body tensing even more with horror. She had to stop this, had to find a way to make it right.

Because no matter how badly she wanted Reece, she couldn't have him. He already belonged to someone else.

CHAPTER NINE

"I'VE GOT TO GO to California."

The words echoed in the kitchen, and for long moments Sarah's brain simply wouldn't comprehend what Reece was telling her. It had been a long night, one she'd spent dozing upright in the rocking chair, a fitful Rose in her arms. Every time she'd thought the baby was in a deep sleep and had tried to put her in the crib, Rose had woken screaming, her hands clutching desperately at Sarah. She'd finally concluded the baby was getting sick and had abandoned all attempts to put her down. Instead, Sarah caught whatever sleep she could sitting upright holding Rose.

She'd heard Reece going to bed some time after eleven. His footsteps had hesitated outside the closed door of the nursery for long, heart-wrenching seconds before continuing on.

And she had known that he was as unsettled by what had happened as she was. That he was as conflicted. And she had known, even then, that he would attempt to back away as far and as fast as he could.

But an unplanned business trip nearly two thousand miles away? Surely that was taking things too far.

"When did this come up?" she asked as she poured herself a large mug of coffee and took a long, slow slip. It didn't wake up her foggy brain, but it did chase the worst of the cobwebs away.

"Matt called this morning. Said things were falling apart at the site and that the situation needs my touch." He wouldn't meet her eyes, might as well have been talking to the wall for all the attention that he paid her.

Anger built. She tried to shove it down. To ignore it. After all, it wouldn't change anything and it certainly would not get her the answers she needed.

"When are you leaving?" She continued to watch him over the rim of her cup, even knowing that it made him uncomfortable. Maybe because she knew it did.

"This morning." He glanced at his watch. "I've got an eleven o'clock flight."

He was a fast worker. As it was already after eight, he'd have to leave for the airport in the next fifteen minutes. Which left no time for questions. No time for arguments or recriminations. She took another sip of coffee, struggled to hold on to her calm demeanor.

"How long will you be gone?"

"I don't know." He dumped his uneaten cereal down the garbage disposal, then used the noise as an excuse to avoid talking to her.

When he turned around, his eyes were distant, his face carefully blank. "Two weeks," he said. "Maybe three, if it's not an easy fix."

Three weeks? Confirmation that the trip was an

excuse to get out of an uncomfortable situation. An excuse to get away from her.

A chill swept through her despite the hot temperature outside. He was walking out, leaving them. He hadn't said the words, but she recognized the signs. She'd been here before. *I'll be gone a couple of weeks.* Famous last words.

Her father's voice echoed in her head, blending with her husband's. The couple of weeks had turned into months, then years, until Sarah had forgotten what they'd looked like. What had made her think she should expect more for her children? It wasn't like she hadn't been anticipating this.

That was the kicker. She *had* known better, had told herself this very thing would happen when Reece had moved in months ago. Had spent the first two months waiting for the slam of the door behind him.

But he'd convinced her that he wasn't like that, had taken such an interest in her sons and their daughter that she had let herself believe. That she had let herself think maybe, just maybe, he wouldn't walk away from them as casually as her parents had walked away from her.

She'd been wrong and had only herself to blame. She pictured the boys' confused faces when they learned that Uncle Reece had left without saying goodbye. She pictured them waiting for him to come back, clinging to the hope only children could have.

Her children didn't deserve this—she didn't deserve this. They had done nothing but open their hearts to him and he was cutting at the first sign of trouble? What a coward. If it wasn't for the children, she'd be damned glad to be rid of him.

"Well, if—"

"Sarah, I—"

They spoke at once and both stopped after the first few awkward words. When he didn't speak, she said, "You should probably go. Traffic's bad in the morning and you don't want to miss your flight."

Reece studied the wall behind her head. "You're probably right." He started to turn away then stopped. "I'm sorry. I know the timing of this trip is crappy."

"Not really. I think it will be a good break—for both of us." She was proud of how even her voice was, how calm, when what she really wanted to do was rage at him. But she forced a smile, even managed a small pat to his shoulder. "Well, take care. Have a safe flight."

"I'll call you." His voice was low, uncertain. One small corner of her brain registered just how unusual that was, but the rage blinded her against trying to figure out what that uncertainty meant.

"You don't have to." She started up the stairs.

"I mean, to check on Rose. And the boys."

For how long? she wanted to demand. For a few days? A few weeks? Until he forgot they existed? How long could she expect him to remember to pick up the phone?

"Of course. I'm sure they'd like to hear your voice."

"All right, then." He picked up his suitcase—his very large, very bulky suitcase that reinforced that he was planning for a long stay. "I'll talk to you soon."

"Sure." She paused at the top of the steps and looked down at him. "Good luck."

"Sarah—"

"I've got to take a shower," she said, "or I'll be late for my client appointment."

"Oh, shit. I was supposed to babysit Rose."

"Don't worry about it. I'll think of something."

"Think of what?"

"It's not your problem." She pointed to the clock. "You need to go."

His eyes followed her finger. "I'm sorry, Sarah."

"Don't worry about it. I certainly won't."

She walked into her bedroom without another backward glance, closing the door behind her. Less than a minute later she heard the front door open and close. Tears welled in her eyes, but she refused to shed them. Instead, she wrapped her arms around herself and sank to the floor. She concentrated on taking deep breaths, telling herself that as long as she was breathing she wouldn't fall apart.

But it was a lie. She could feel her heart—already so fragile—crack in half at Reece's departure.

HE FELT LIKE A TOTAL ASSHOLE. The look on Sarah's face as she'd climbed the stairs haunted Reece still, nearly two weeks after he'd run away from her like the coward he hadn't known he was.

But what was he supposed to do? Stay when he wanted her so badly he could barely see straight? Take her when he wasn't ready to take anyone, let alone his

wife's best friend? Use her when she'd already given—
and given up—so much?

What other choice had he had but to leave? If he'd
remained in that house with her and the kids, he would
have made love to her. And she would have let him.
Maybe not that night or the next, but soon, when the
hormones and the emotions were too much for them.

Then where would they be? Their friendship ruined,
the arrangement they had destroyed. And for what?
Some great sex that went nowhere? No, he assured
himself as he slowly got dressed, he had done the right
thing. Even if it hadn't looked like it from his spot in
the cheap seats.

Sarah had been devastated, his rejection hurting her
much more than he'd dreamed possible. She hadn't
wanted to hear his explanations. He had called her
numerous times but had only spoken to her twice. And
on those occasions, she had let the boys do most of the
talking, claiming that Rose had a cold and she was busy
taking care of her.

Frustration ate at him until he felt like a wild animal
in a trap—unable to find a way out and willing to chew
off his own foot in order to escape. He wanted her to
understand that he'd done what he had to protect her.

"Are you ready?" Matt poked his head into the
living area of the two-bedroom suite their clients had
put them up at. "We're going to be late for dinner."

"Yeah. Let me grab a jacket. I'm still not used to how
cold it is in this city."

"It's San Francisco." Matt had his own jacket over

his arm and headed for the door. "You should be grateful we're not suffering through the hundred-degree heat that's still swamping Austin, man."

"I guess." Reece checked to make sure he had his keycard and wallet before following his partner into the hall.

"Well I, for one, am enjoying it. I was just at Fisherman's Wharf—that place is so cool."

"You think anywhere there's water is cool."

"Well, yeah. I still can't believe you land locked me in the middle of Texas. We so should have set up business somewhere near a beach."

"So you could surf all day and I could do all the work?"

"There a problem with that?" Matt shot him a well-duh look that would normally have had him grinning, but today Reece couldn't work up even a twitch of his lips.

"Hey, what's going on?" Matt asked. "You look worse than you have in months."

"I don't know. Tired, I guess."

"With all the tossing and turning you do at night, it's no wonder."

It was his turn to shoot Matt a look. "How do you know whether I'm tossing or turning at night?"

"Thin walls, man." Matt held up his hands in a peace-making gesture. "Your room is right next to mine."

"I kissed Sarah." The words were out before he could stop them and Reece shuddered as he awaited his friend's reaction.

"No kidding, really?" Matt's eyebrows shot up as they stepped onto the empty elevator. "When?"

"Ten days—"

"Of course. That's why you came running out here like a cat with its tail on fire. I thought it was 'cause you didn't trust me."

Reece didn't bother to grace that comment with an answer—he knew exactly how warped Matt's sense of humor was. "I needed to get away from her for a while."

"It was that bad?" Matt stared at him incredulously as they made their way through the lobby. "I can't believe that. Sarah is fine!"

Reece punched him in the arm. "I swear, you still think like a frat boy."

"Hey, once a Pike, always a Pike."

"Well, grow up. It's not that it was bad—"

"So it was good?"

"Why do I even bother to talk to you? It's like conversing with a sixteen-year-old."

"What does it say about you, then, that I'm the best friend you've got?"

"I shudder to imagine." Reece kept his voice dry, but the truth was Matt's antics were lifting his mood—exactly as his friend had probably intended. Reece still wanted to put his fist through the nearest wall, but at least the urgency was gone.

"So seriously, then," Matt said as he climbed into the driver's seat of the black Lexus he had rented. The guy had a serious thing for black cars—refused to drive anything else because of the cool factor. "What has you so freaked out? She's a beautiful woman, you're an okay-looking guy. You've already got a kid together. Seems like a match made in heaven."

"She's Vanessa's best friend." Reece stared at him in disbelief. How was it that Matt couldn't figure out what was stressful about the situation? But then a look at his friend's face told him not only had Matt figured it out, but also he wanted to downplay it as much as possible.

The car fell silent for a few minutes.

"Vanessa's dead, Reece. She isn't coming back," Matt said quietly.

It took all his self-control not to punch Matt. "I'm well aware of that. More so, I think, than you are."

"I didn't mean it like that, Reece. I meant, you have a daughter who needs her mother and two little boys who look up to you like a father. Would it be so bad—"

"It hasn't even been a year yet."

"I know that." Matt fixed his hands on the wheel. "But will it be better in a year or two? After Sarah's given up on you and moved on to someone else?"

"You don't know what the hell you're talking about."

"Don't I? Reece, she's a beautiful, intelligent woman with two little boys who need a father. How long do you think it'll be before she goes shopping for one?"

"Sarah's not like that." God help him if she was, because he could scarcely control the jealousy at the mere thought of her looking at another man.

"Like what? From what you've told me, her husband left six years ago. Why wouldn't she want to get married again?"

"Not to me."

"Why not you?"

"Because my wife just died. Because she was Sarah's best friend. Because of Rose and all the complications in this whole stinking situation." He took a deep breath, tried to calm himself.

"Being with Sarah reminds me of Vanessa. It reinforces her loss, but also the relationship we once had. Sarah was her friend. For years, that's the only way I've ever let myself look at her."

"Hey, whoa, what does that mean? *Let* yourself?"

Trust Matt to get to the heart of the matter. He might look like a surfer and sound like a frat boy, but he had a mind like a ninja—highly disciplined, completely flexible and full of twists and turns that let him see the big picture better than anyone Reece had ever met.

"It means I've always had a thing for Sarah, ever since the first time I met her." The words burst from him, and he couldn't tell who was more shocked—Matt or him.

"Wow." Matt stopped at a red light and turned to stare at him incredulously. "How did I have no idea about this?"

"When I first met her, she was married and I was dating Van. It was completely inappropriate. Then she was divorced and I was married—still inappropriate."

"And now?" Matt asked softly.

The question hung there for what felt like forever. "Do you know what it's like to want your wife's best friend? To try to build a life with one woman while a tiny part of you is always wondering about another? I loved Vanessa and tried to be a good husband to her, but if I do this—" He let the words trail off, unwilling to voice his true fears.

"If you do this, then it's like you never loved Vanessa at all."

Reece stared out the passenger side window as the words stabbed like knives. He didn't answer, but then he didn't have to. Matt had hit the nail on the head and they both knew it.

"I loved Vanessa very much, and I never once thought of cheating on her." Reece swallowed, forcing the words past the lump lodged in his throat. "But sometimes I couldn't help comparing her to Sarah. Sarah was so much stronger and bolder than Vanessa could ever be. So much more straightforward and easygoing. And—" His voice broke. "And I wished, more than once, that Vanessa was more like her. More of a fighter. More passionate. More willing to stand on her own."

He stared at his friend. "So you tell me. How can being with Sarah now be *anything* but a total betrayal of my wife?"

CHAPTER TEN

TERROR WAS a living, breathing animal inside of Sarah as she raced into the emergency room, Rose's too-still body in her arms. "My baby can't breathe!" The words poured out of her. "Help me, please. She can't breathe."

She was immediately surrounded by medical personnel.

"Is she choking?"

"No. She's had a cold, but her breathing got really labored. And when we were in the car, she started turning blue. I got here as fast as I could."

Sarah could feel the absolute panic that was one slip of her control away. She barely had the presence of mind to relinquish her daughter to the care of the nurses.

Rose, please don't die.

Please don't leave me, baby.

Two nurses had whisked Rose to the treatment area. One was flicking the bottom of Rose's foot with her index finger while the other was calling for a doctor.

Fighting back her fear, trying to be strong as they slipped an oxygen mask over her baby's mouth, Sarah hovered out of the way even as she murmured wordlessly to Rose. If her baby was going to die— No. She wasn't going down that road. Not now. Not ever.

Rose would be fine. Rose would be—Sarah cried out at Rose's pitiful attempts to scream as the nurses put an IV into her too-tiny hand. The baby lacked the breath to offer much resistance. Even with the oxygen pumping into her she was too pale, too blue.

"What brought this on?" the doctor snapped out as she rushed into the cubicle.

"She's had a cold for a week and a half and she just isn't getting better." Sarah repeated the same information she'd given the nurses. "I've taken her to the doctor three times and today the doctor gave her this inhaler." She fumbled in her purse for the albuterol inhaler her pediatrician had prescribed to combat Rose's sudden onset of wheezing.

"Was she premature?" the doctor asked.

Sarah shook her head. "Only by a couple of weeks, but it was negligible. She was in great shape and she came home with me. She was fine. She was fine," she repeated.

No one was listening. One nurse fit a pulse ox monitor onto Rose's chubby toes, while the other one injected the IV with something.

The doctor had her stethoscope in her ears and was listening to Rose's too-labored breathing.

"What's wrong with her?" Sarah demanded. "What are you giving her?"

"Your baby's lungs are filled with fluid," one of the nurses answered soothingly. "We're giving her something to get rid of some of it so she can breathe easier."

"But what's wrong with her? Why is this happening? I've taken her to the doctor." Even as she spoke, Sarah knew her voice was all wrong. Too high-pitched. Too scared. But try as she might, she couldn't regulate it. Like her heartbeat and the terror rocketing through her, it was beyond her control.

Don't die, Rose. Don't die. Don't die. It was a mantra— a prayer and a plea. A demand and a declaration. She couldn't lose Rose. Not now. She knew there was no way she would survive it.

After what felt like an eternity, the doctor turned to her, her stethoscope dangling around her neck. "Rose is obviously very sick. My first instinct is to say pneumonia, but I'm going to get a chest X ray and do some blood work to be sure."

"Pneumonia?" Sarah stared at the woman blankly. "But we were at the doctor today and he said she was okay. He said the cold was only hanging on longer than normal. How could he be so wrong?"

"He might not have been." The doctor—Dr. Adams, according to her name tag—laid a soothing hand on Sarah's shoulder. Or at least she assumed it was supposed to be soothing, though it was anything but. Her experience with E.R. doctors up to this point had proven that the nicer they were, the worse the news they had to deliver.

She found herself wishing for a brusque, rude doctor. An impatient doctor. A doctor who had more important patients to see. Anyone or anything but this doctor staring at her with a grave expression and concerned eyes.

"Babies can get sick very quickly. They can go from normal to dangerously ill in just a few hours." Dr. Adams glanced at Rose. "Is this your first one?"

"No." Sarah clutched Rose's baby blanket to her chest. "She's my third." She barely got the words past her chattering teeth, but no one seemed to notice.

"Then you know what I'm talking about." Dr. Adams smiled. "The upshot of that quick descent to illness is that the recovery time can be almost as quick."

Sarah grasped her words like a lifeline. "Is that what's going to happen to Rose? Is she going to be okay now?"

Rose's color had improved minimally, but she was too quiet, her breathing still too heavy. She was retracting badly, her little stomach getting sucked in behind her ribs as she struggled for oxygen.

"We'll take this an hour at a time, all right?" The doctor reached for her chart. "For right now, why don't you sit down next to the bed? The nurses will take some blood and I'm going to order the X ray right now. Someone should be here in a few minutes and we'll talk after I get a better idea of what's going on."

Sarah was painfully aware of the fact that the doctor hadn't given her the reassurance she had so desperately sought, but didn't push it. Don't ask the question if you can't handle the answer—that's what her favorite teacher had often preached.

"Can I hold her?"

"Of course." The tall nurse answered, her smile gentle as she took blood from Rose, using the arm that didn't have the IV in it. The baby was so exhausted that she didn't even flinch. "Just let me finish here then I'll hand her to you."

Moments later the nurse did just that and Sarah nearly wept at the sweetness of having her daughter in her arms, Rose's small, sturdy body curled against her chest.

"Careful of the IV. You don't want to pull on it or we'll have to start all over again."

"I'll be careful."

The woman's smile was kind. "I know you will. I'll get this blood to the lab then I'll be back to get your information."

Sarah nodded as her own eyes drifted shut. She wondered how Tad and Pamela were doing with the boys, but let the worry go. Her brother would call her if there was a problem. Right now, Rose needed her.

The next few hours passed in a blur of questions and insurance information and tests. X rays, blood tests, breathing tests, another X ray, an ultrasound. It went on and on until Sarah wanted to scream. Until she wanted to beg for someone to tell her what was wrong with her daughter. For someone to tell her how she could make Rose all right again. At one point, she did call Tad and check in; he assured her the boys were sound asleep in his guest room.

The knowledge that part of her family was okay soothed her, helped her get through the rest of the insanely long night.

Finally, as the clock on the wall ticked toward 5:00 a.m., Dr. Adams came back.

"What is it?" Sarah demanded, the prolonged panic

cutting through any and all politeness she might have had. "What's wrong with my daughter?"

Her arms were numb from holding her daughter in the upright position that seemed to make breathing easier for Rose, but not for a second did she consider letting her go. Putting her down.

"Rose has a very bad case of viral pneumonia, complicated by a lung infection that's gone undiagnosed."

"Viral?" Sarah questioned as a fist grabbed her heart and began to squeeze. "But that means antibiotics won't…" Her voice trailed off as her worst nightmares became reality.

"You're right. Antibiotics probably won't work. But we're going to start her on a course of them to take care of the lung infection. We don't want her catching anything else—her immune system is severely compromised at this point and we don't want any secondary infections to crop up."

"So how do we treat the pneumonia? How do we make her better?"

"That's a tricky question at the best of times and it's made trickier because of the fact that your daughter is still an infant. But there are some things we can do to make her more comfortable and get her on track to recovery."

The doctor proceeded to outline her suggested course of treatment and Sarah listened to every word with the most intense concentration she could muster. Not only because she needed to know, but also because when she finally got a break she would have to call Reece.

She wasn't looking forward to the task.

When they were finally settled in their cubical in the infant intensive care unit and Rose was sleeping fitfully—her breathing was calm if not even—Sarah collapsed in the chair beside the bed and let the tears she'd been holding in all night slowly leak out. She wanted to scream, to sob, to rage at the world about the unfairness of it all. Why her baby girl?

She gave herself ten minutes. Ten minutes to cry, ten minutes to whine about the unfairness. Ten minutes to get her own emotions under control so she could make the calls she knew she had to make.

When she no longer felt a hitch in her throat, she called Tad. As soon as he picked up the phone she could hear the boys laughing in the background.

"I assume that means the boys are doing okay?" she asked, relief coursing through her.

"They're doing great. Pam had an early meeting, so I'm making pancakes before I take the boys to school."

"Thank you, Tad. I don't know what I would do without you."

"Don't worry about it. That's what I'm here for. Hold on—" There were a few seconds of silence and then she heard, "Who gets the first airplane pancake?"

"Me, me," came a chorus of shouts from the boys and she couldn't help smiling. Bless Johnny and Justin for sparking something she'd worried she'd never do again.

"You still there, sis?" Tad came back on the line.

"I am. I packed clothes for them in their backpacks, so—"

"Already found them. The boys are dressed, hair combed, teeth brushed.'

"Aren't you the efficient one this morning?"

"You only say that because you can't see the disaster that is my house at this very moment."

"I owe you one, Tad."

"Don't worry. I'll collect when you least expect it."

"Somehow, I knew that."

"So, how's Rose?" Tad's voice turned quiet.

"She's got viral pneumonia, so they're starting a course of treatment. She'll be in ICU for the next few days and we'll go from there."

"Geez, I'm sorry, Sarah."

A sob tickled the back of her throat, but she forced it down. "She'll be okay."

"Of course she will. Let me get the boys to school and I'll come sit with you."

"No, I'm fine. I don't want you to miss work."

"Sarah—"

"Please, go to work. If you come, I'll just fall apart and I don't want to do that."

There was a long pause. "Are you sure?"

Again she fought to keep back the tears. "Yes."

"I'll bring the boys by after school—they'll want to see you."

"That'd be great."

"I love you, sis."

"Oh, Tad, I love you, too."

Another long pause, as if Tad couldn't bring himself

to hang up. Finally, he said, "Are you sure you don't want me to come?"

"I'm positive." She glanced at her watch. "Now get the boys to school. If you don't leave soon, they're going to be late."

"We're on our way."

"Okay, then. Bye." Sarah forced herself to hang up the phone, forced herself to let go of the one small piece of security she had in her life. When her father left, when Mike left, when Van died, Tad had always been there for her. No matter how bad his own life had been, he'd always stood up for her.

Taking a deep breath, she studied the phone in her hand much as she would a viper's nest. She couldn't put it off any longer. She had to call Reece, and she needed to do it now so that her mind would be clear when Rose woke again.

REECE NEARLY THREW his cell phone across the room when it started to ring again. He was exhausted, utterly worn-out from dealing with this job and still trying to handle all the other clients, as well. He'd been on the phone until after three trying to resolve a problem with the project in Hawaii and it was now—he squinted at the clock on the nightstand—only 6:00 a.m.

Rolling over, he buried his head under his pillow and tried to ignore the ringing phone. He breathed a sigh of relief when the shrill rings stopped, then groaned as they started almost instantaneously.

He frowned as he picked up the phone—the number

was unfamiliar. He answered it anyway, barking, "Hello?" in the nastiest voice he could manage. If it was a wrong number, he'd—

"Reece? It's Sarah."

Fear whipped through his veins at the sound of her voice. "What's wrong?" The way he had left things between them, there was no way Sarah would be calling him if there wasn't a problem, especially not before dawn California time.

"It's Ro—" Her voice cracked and his fear turned to ice-cold panic.

"What's wrong with Rose?" The phone grew slippery beneath his palm. "Is she all right?"

The ten seconds it took Sarah to answer him stretched to eternity. "She's in the hospital."

"Tell me."

And she did. He reeled at the images of Rose gasping for breath, her little body turning blue from lack of oxygen. Nearly lost it completely when Sarah mentioned the intensive care unit.

"I'll get on the first flight out."

"You don't have to do that. We've got things under control—"

"My daughter is in the hospital." He couldn't stop the frigid whip of his voice. Didn't know if he even wanted to. "Where else would I be?"

"Of course. I'm sorry."

"I'll call you when I have my flight information— give you a better idea of when I'll be there."

"Okay. Thanks."

He started to hang up then remembered. "Hey, how are the boys?"

"They're okay. My brother has them right now." Again her voice broke.

He couldn't be upset with her for a second longer. "Hang in there, Sarah. I'll be there as soon as I can."

He hung up the phone then leaped into action, his exhaustion forgotten as adrenaline raced through him. He pulled up the morning flights on his laptop, found one leaving in a little over an hour. If he packed quickly, he should be able to make it.

Throwing on the first clothes he touched, he dumped the rest of his stuff in his suitcase, in between trips to the bathroom to brush his teeth and pack up his toiletries. As he packed, his mind whirled a million miles a minute. He'd have to cancel the conference call he had set up with Hawaii for this afternoon, have to get Matt to cover the meetings he had this morning.

Within fifteen minutes, he'd booked his flight, filled his partner in on the situation and was in a cab to the airport. And it wasn't until he was sitting in the back of the cab, with nothing to do but think, that the worst hit him.

He could lose Rose.

She was sick, so sick that Sarah said the doctor's weren't making any guarantees. They said it was good that Sarah had gotten her to the hospital so soon, but viral pneumonia was almost untreatable for a baby. Antibiotics didn't work. All the medical people could do was keep Rose comfortable and hydrated.

A chill unlike anything he'd ever felt crept through

him. Could this really be happening? He'd scarcely survived losing Vanessa. Was he going to have to lose Rose, too—now that he was attached to her? Now that he loved her so much he couldn't imagine a world without her in it?

With shame, he thought back to the last months of Sarah's pregnancy. To the first months of Rose's life. He hadn't been there for her. Had been too wrapped up in his selfish grief and petty insecurities to get off his ass and see his daughter. God, would those paltry few weeks living in Sarah's house be all he'd ever have with Rose?

Without conscious thought, he opened his wallet to the small wedding picture of Vanessa and him that he kept there. She looked so beautiful in the photo, so pretty and happy. They had both been ready to take the world by storm that day. They'd graduated from college two weeks earlier and had planned to start their new jobs as soon as they returned from the honeymoon. He had a position as an apprentice architect at one of the oldest and most respected firms in Dallas and she was starting as an assistant chef at one of the area's finest restaurants. They'd had it all.

For so long, things had been great. Wonderful. Amazing. She'd supported him when he and Matt had decided to open their own firm. He'd been thrilled when she'd been promoted to sous-chef, even though it meant much longer hours—often at night, when he was finished for the day.

And though it was hard, they'd managed to stick it out. Had managed to keep things nice and relaxed and romantic—up until Vanessa decided it was time for them to have a baby. Then things had gone to hell, fast.

After six months with no results, she'd dragged them to fertility expert after fertility expert—and each had told them the same thing. Vanessa had severe scarring on her fallopian tubes due to endometriosis and would likely never be able to conceive a child. Surgery might help increase her chances, but even that was no guarantee.

He'd tried to explain to Van that a child didn't matter to him. That, while he would love any baby they did have, the idea of not having a child didn't fill him with regret. He loved her, not her ability to reproduce.

She hadn't heard him. She was so crazed to have a baby that he doubted she heard anything anyone had to tell her. Three surgeries and four years later they still hadn't had a baby and their marriage was in a precarious state. It had grown even more so when she hit on the idea of having Sarah help her have a baby.

He'd argued against the scheme until he had no words left. But Vanessa had remained determined. Finally worn down, he'd agreed—to keep the peace, and as a last-ditch effort to keep his marriage together. Sarah had conceived, almost effortlessly. Vanessa was convinced it was a sign, that this baby was meant to be. And for a while, he'd let himself believe it. After all, his wife was happy again, excited, like the woman he'd married. He'd allowed himself to get excited—about her, about the baby, about their future together. That excitement had sustained him until the state troopers knocked on his door late one night and told him that his wife was dead.

Everything had gone to hell. He fell apart and lost himself in a morass of self-pity. He was a failure, a man who couldn't help his wife get over her obsession. A man who'd agreed to have a baby to keep the peace, not out of any desire to be a father. A man who had been unable to keep his wife alive, even when she'd had everything to live for.

Oh, he'd gone to work every day. But only because staying home meant staying with the memories of how he'd failed Vanessa. He'd stayed in that emotional void, feeling sorry for himself—hating himself—until the moment he had first laid eyes on Rose.

He'd never regretted stepping up and becoming her father—he only regretted the delay in making that decision. It had never occurred to him that his precious baby girl might not even see her first birthday.

He wanted to howl, to beg, to pray—but he'd given up praying when his wife had died. Instead, he stared out the window as the cab whisked through the early-morning streets of San Francisco and thought of Rose.

Thought of her sweet smell and her even sweeter smiles. Thought of the temper that was emerging and the stubbornness that had been there all along.

He thought of her so hard and long that he could almost believe things would work out all right. Almost.

CHAPTER ELEVEN

IT HAD BEEN one of the longest days of Sarah's life and it was only a little more than half-over. Glancing at the clock for what felt like the fiftieth time, she was disheartened to see only five minutes had passed since she'd last looked.

But it was still only two-thirty. The boys weren't even out of school yet, hadn't had time to miss her or wonder where she was. Thank God. She didn't know what she was going to do about them after today. Tad had volunteered to take them again with him—for which she was eternally grateful.

But it was a quick fix. The doctor had warned her that Rose would be in here at least four or five days, more if the virus persisted.

Sarah couldn't keep imposing on her brother. He and his wife both worked full-time and it wasn't right to ask them to take time off to watch her children. When she'd said as much, Tad had laughed at her, told her that this was what family was for.

In her head, she knew he was right, remembered Vanessa saying the same thing to her more than once when she'd asked her friend for help. But she'd spent the majority of her life not depending on anyone. Not counting on anyone to be there when she faltered. A lesson learned so early in life was not one she was likely to forget.

Yet she caught herself anticipating Reece's arrival as if he were a life line. He hadn't called her back, as promised, to tell her when his flight was coming in, but she wasn't surprised. Between the rush to get to the hospital and his obvious worry over Rose, she would be amazed if he could still remember his own name.

She glanced at the clock again—two thirty-seven. If he'd managed to get a flight soon after she'd called him, then he should be close.

What would she say to him? How could she explain that she had let their little girl get this sick without doing something about it. Without notifying him.

How did this happen, Sarah?

She could still hear the disbelief—and the blame— echoing over the phone line. She had told him what the doctor said—about babies getting sick so quickly—but she could tell he didn't believe her. She wouldn't have believed it if she hadn't seen it herself. If she hadn't taken Rose to the doctor that very morning. If Sarah hadn't seen her little girl playing with her blocks in the middle of the family room mere hours before her breathing had become so labored.

A sob threatened to escape, but Sarah fought it back. She wouldn't do this, she wouldn't break down now when Rose needed her to be strong. Sarah had already had her ten minutes. The rest would have to wait, no matter how sad she was.

She sought distraction by focusing on the activity in the hallway. She heard the doctor talking to the parents in the room next door, knew that he was doing his rounds. Sarah heard shoes squeaking on the tile, telephones ringing, the nurses' voices blending together at the nurses' station. Then the heavy thud of shoes rushing closer.

Reece.

Jumping up, she swiped at her hair. She refused to greet him disheveled and fragile. Maybe it was pride, maybe it was guilt—she didn't know and she didn't care.

He was here.

Sarah's mind shut down as Reece turned the corner into Rose's tiny room. She couldn't move, couldn't think. Couldn't breathe. Then he reached for her, pulled her against him and held her with one arm, while he reached out the other one to Rose.

"How is she?" His voice was hoarse as he ran a hand over Rose's nearly bald head.

"She's breathing a little easier, but there doesn't seem to be much change. The doctor's doing rounds now, though. He should be here in a few minutes."

"Is this the pediatric pulmonologist?"

"No, they say he'll stop by later today. This is the regular doctor—the one we got after she was admitted from the E.R." It took all her strength to lock her knees so she wouldn't sink into Reece. He had enough to deal with right now—he didn't need her to lose it on top of everything else.

But he felt so good pressed against her, so steady and

in control. Everything that she wasn't. His presence alone made her believe everything would be okay. That Rose would get better.

"Your daddy's here, sweetheart." She leaned over and pressed a kiss to the sleeping baby's forehead. "He came back just for you, so you need to fight, okay? You need to get better so he can take you to the park and—" The words jammed behind the lump in her throat.

"Sarah." Reece's voice—so calm and familiar— calmed her, prevented her from spiraling out of control.

"Come sit down." He gestured toward the chair next to the bed. "You look like you're about to fall down."

"I'm fine."

"You're not fine." He shoved the second chair close and took a seat himself. "Now, sit and tell me about our daughter. I want to know everything that you know."

The snap of command in his voice was so unexpected— so shocking—that Sarah found herself staring at him with her mouth open even as she took a seat.

SHE LOOKED LIKE HELL. The thought ran through Reece's head as he watched Sarah. As bad as she had all those months ago when he'd shown up at her door.

She might even look worse because today her tiredness ran second to the sadness and worry. Sarah was on edge, close to breaking, and he'd been two thousand miles away, oblivious to anyone else's needs but his own.

"How long has she been sick?" he asked, keeping his voice low.

"Since the day you left. Remember how much trouble she'd had settling the night before? It was because she wasn't feeling well."

He did remember, just as he remembered pausing outside Rose's door and debating whether to go in. It had been obvious that Sarah was having trouble getting Rose down, but instead of helping, he'd walked away. Too lost in his dilemma about kissing Sarah to think about her or his daughter. Too selfish to put them first.

God, he really was a bastard.

But he was here now. That had to count for something. Not much, maybe, but something. "You took her to the doctor?"

"Of course I took her to the doctor." If possible, Sarah's back got even straighter. "I took her to the doctor three times and each time he told me to wait it out. That she would get better, but it would take a while. That she wasn't getting worse and that was the important thing."

"But she was getting worse."

"This last time, yes. Which is why he gave me the inhaler and told me to bring her back the next day if there was no progress. But by the time night fell, I knew she couldn't wait until morning. So I brought her here."

Reece nodded, kept his face composed when he really wanted to beg her forgiveness. Beg Rose's forgiveness. "I should have been here."

"Why?" The look she shot him was full of surprise and somehow made him feel a million times worse. She sure knew how to hit a guy where it hurt.

"I could have helped." He gestured to Rose. "It

couldn't have been easy taking care of a sick baby on top of Justin and Johnny."

"I managed."

He gritted his teeth, managed to shove down the impulse to strangle her. Barely. "I know you managed. I was just saying you shouldn't have had to. I should have been there to help out."

"You had work. I understand that. Besides, it's not like we're married, right?"

It was his turn to stiffen. That was a shot Vanessa would have taken. It put his back up like nothing else could have. "Do you really think this is the time for that?"

"For what?" she asked, her expression baffled.

"I know you're mad at me for leaving, but you don't need to rub it in my face."

"Reece, do you really think that's what I'm doing?" Reaching over, she took his hand, the first voluntary gesture she'd made toward him since he'd entered the room. "I'm not angry with you. I was only saying, I don't expect you to be at my beck and call. You have a life and I am more than aware of that. You couldn't have known this would happen. I just hope you're not angry at me. I thought I was doing the right things for her."

"Sarah—" A knock at the door cut him off. He actually felt Sarah sag with relief when she saw the white-coated man standing near the door.

"How's she doing?" the doctor asked. "Any better?"

If this was the doctor shouldn't *he* be telling them how Rose was doing instead of the other way around?

Because in Reece's opinion, his little girl wasn't doing well at all. When he'd left a week and a half ago she'd been a bouncing bundle of energy and life and now each breath she took seemed a torturous, impossible event.

He wanted to rail at the doctor, to demand that he do more. But seeing as how Reece had just gotten there and had no idea what Rose had looked like the night before, he figured he wasn't the one who should be opening his mouth. Yet Sarah's instant snap to attention irritated him no end. The man was a doctor, not a god.

"I don't know, Dr. Marino. Her breathing isn't as labored as it was last night, but she's exhausted. She sleeps all the time, and she hasn't wanted to eat, though the nurses and I keep trying to feed her."

The doctor nodded as he picked up the baby's chart and began to read the nurse's notes. "That's to be expected, Sarah. Think about how you feel when you're sick. That tiredness and unwillingness to eat is the same with her—worse, because she doesn't understand how necessary fluids are for her." He nodded to the IV. "But she's getting everything she needs through that."

Reece wasn't convinced. He didn't like this guy's nonchalance, any more than he liked the warm way the guy was regarding Sarah. As if the two of them had become friends in the twelve hours it had taken Reece to fly in from San Francisco.

Part of him wanted to beat his chest and roar. To tell buddy doctor to back off—that Sarah was his woman and Rose was his daughter and that neither were up for grabs. But Reece kept his mouth shut. Liking Rose's doctor wasn't a prerequisite. As long as he helped make her better, he could be evil incarnate himself for all Reece cared.

"So, are you little Rose's father?" The doctor looked at him as if sizing up the competition—and finding him lacking.

"Yes." Reese managed to get out the word through gritted teeth.

"It's good to see you here. The flight from San Francisco must have been a long one."

Exactly what did he mean by that? Reece had gotten here as soon as he possibly could. But the doctor's face showed such benign interest that Reece shoved his dark thoughts to the back of his mind, even as he reminded himself—again—that it was Rose who was important.

"So, how is she?" He nodded toward his sleeping daughter.

"Her chart looks good. She seems to be responding to the medicine. But I'll know more once I examine her."

He stepped closer to the bed and placed his stethoscope on her chest. Then, to Reece's surprise, the doctor ran a hand over Rose's head and murmured, "Wake up, sweet Rose. Wake up, baby girl."

Rose whimpered in her sleep, her little fist going to her mouth as it always did when she needed comfort.

"Why are you waking her? I thought she needed her sleep."

The look the doctor shot him was half-amused and

half-annoyed. "She does. But I want to see if she's got the energy to fuss or if she's as lethargic as she was last night."

Reece watched—jaws and hands clenched—as the doctor continued to annoy Rose and she began to whimper. She didn't let loose with any full-fledged yells, as he'd expected her to, but the soft whines she did produce were ten times as heartbreaking.

Beside him, he could sense Sarah anxiously watching their daughter, her shoulders sagging a little more with each whimper.

"She's not crying," he said softly, his hand seeking hers unconsciously. He needed comfort as he watched his baby struggle.

"She hasn't been able to cry," Sarah whispered. "Dr. Marino says it isn't that abnormal for babies in Rose's condition. It's good for her to save her energy for getting well."

"Is that true?" Reece pinned the doctor with a look that demanded the truth. He would brook no hedging or half-truths.

"It is true." Dr. Marino nodded his head. "But I was hoping for a little more response this late in the day."

"What does that mean?" Sarah's nails dug into the back of Reece's hand.

"Nothing terrible," the doctor answered soothingly. "It simply means that she's taking a little longer to respond to the treatment than we had hoped."

"Is she—" Reece couldn't voice the question that had been on his mind since he'd received Sarah's call.

"We don't know what's going to happen," the doctor

said. "But I'm heartened by the fact that her breathing is easier and that she does have some fight in her. The lethargy seems to be on its way out."

Relief swept through him at the doctor's words. So much so that Reece found himself taking a kinder stance on the man's obvious interest in his wi—in *Sarah*.

He wasn't really thinking of her like that, he assured himself. He was just confused, emotional, worried about Rose. And Sarah was the mother of his child— it was natural to think of her that way. Normal, even.

Too bad he didn't believe the lies even as he was spinning them. Things had changed between him and Sarah on that couch nearly two weeks ago. Trying to hide from it, to pretend it hadn't happened wasn't going to work. That's what had brought them here, to this place where he hadn't even been around when his daughter became so deathly ill.

They spoke with the doctor for a few more minutes, watched as he closely examined the baby. Then stood awkwardly—looking at everything but each other—as Dr. Marino left.

"Sarah, I'm sorry." The words were out before he knew he was going to speak them.

But she was shaking her head. "We've already been through this—"

"I need to say this." Gathering all of his courage, he searched for the right words to explain something he himself still didn't understand. "I was an ass. A blind, moronic ass. Again. I treated you badly and I am so very, very sorry about that."

"Reece—"

"Let me finish. I got scared. On the couch that night, with you—I got scared."

She stared at him warily. "Why?"

"I wasn't ready. Not just for you, but for any woman. Vanessa was my wife."

"I know that. Things got out of hand."

"Did they?" He studied her for a minute, watched as the afternoon sunlight played over her skin. Lines of exhaustion were clear—evidence of too many sleepless nights. "I don't know about that. But I do know I shouldn't have left you alone like that. Left you to take care of Rose on your own."

He glanced at their sleeping child, watched as she moved restlessly beneath the light blanket. "She's my responsibility, too—as are the boys. And I ran away."

She started to protest, but he stopped her with a gentle hand against her lips. "I want you to know that whatever happens—here with Rose or later, between us—I won't do that to you again. You deserve better and I—" He cleared his throat, forced himself to continue. "I was a coward to leave you."

She didn't respond in any way for long, nerve-racking minutes. Finally, she reached out a hand and stroked it down his cheek. "This is hard for you."

"It's hard for you, too. Van—" He stopped, unable to say his wife's name while he reveled in the touch of another woman.

She seemed to understand, her eyes darkening to the midnight blue of a West Texas sky. "It is hard, but not in the same way. My husband left a long time ago and my loyalty to Vanessa is, obviously, different than yours. But it is okay, Reece. I do understand. I understood when you left. Really."

He wanted to believe her so badly, wanted to accept her words at face value. But Sarah was such a generous person she could easily be putting on a front for him.

Glancing back at his daughter, his heart hurt all over again at how thin and pale she looked. He decided to leave this thing with Sarah alone, to pick it up at a better time. Right now, he figured they had enough to deal with helping their daughter get well.

CHAPTER TWELVE

THE NEXT FEW DAYS passed in a blur of shifts at the hospital with Rose and home with the boys. Sarah and Reece had worked out a schedule so that very rarely were the boys without one of them and Rose never was. Thank God Reece had returned. If this had happened when she was on her own with Rose and Justin and Johnny, Sarah had no idea what she would have done. There was only so much she'd ask Tad to sacrifice and no one else who could put his or her life on hold for the prolonged period it was taking Rose to get well enough to come home.

After Reece's disappearing act, she'd had her doubts about his ability to stick this thing out. But he'd been rock-solid, immovable and perfect to lean on when her emotions, worries and lack of sleep got the best of her.

"Mrs. Martin?"

Sarah glanced up at the now-familiar doctor's voice, but she didn't stop feeding or rocking Rose. Though they'd moved Rose out of the Infant ICU two days ago, today was the first time the baby had shown any interest in her bottles, and Sarah was determined that she get as much formula as her ravenous little body could take.

"She's doing better today," the doctor said with a grin. "The nurses say she's been hungry."

"She's been eating every two hours."

"That's a good sign. The chest X ray they took this morning came back almost completely clear. It looks like she's definitely over the worst."

The relief that swept through her was so acute it was almost pain. Closing her eyes, Sarah murmured a prayer of thanksgiving as she waited to see what else the doctor would say.

"I'd like to keep her one more day, just to ensure she doesn't relapse. But if this progress continues, by this time tomorrow we'll be talking about release."

"Really?" She didn't even try to hide the hope that filled her. "Rose can go home?"

"If things go as planned," he reiterated. "I'm going to run one more blood test to make sure the white blood cell count is reasonably normal, but if her pulse ox and appetite stay where they are today, you'll be free to take her home."

"Thank you. Oh God, thank you so much."

He shook his head. "You're thanking the wrong person. You've got quite a little fighter there. Often in these cases, that's what it comes down to. But you and her father gave her a lot to live for. Sometimes that makes all the difference."

With a smile and a wink he slipped out the door.

If she hadn't been holding a now-dozing Rose, Sarah would have danced around the room in celebration. As it was, she contented herself with burying her face in the curve of Rose's neck and breathing her in. Rose was coming home.

Rose was coming home.

After laying the baby in her crib, she fumbled for the phone. She had to call Reece to tell him the good news. But as she began to dial, a noise behind her alerted her that she wasn't alone. Turning, she saw him standing there.

Dropping the phone, she went to him. Wrapped herself around his shuddering body and held on for all she was worth. And in that one perfect moment, as joy and relief streamed between them, all was as it should be.

"IS SHE ASLEEP?" Sarah asked Reece nearly a week later, as he came into the kitchen where she was washing dishes.

"She is. Like a baby." He grinned at her as he grabbed a towel and began to dry the pans. "I meant to ask, when did the dishwasher break?"

"A couple days after you went to San Francisco. The boys decided their action figures needed to fight a hurricane."

Reece laughed, the sound sending a little frisson of desire just below her skin. "Who won?"

"No one." She tried to keep her voice matter-of-fact. Reminding herself of all the reasons it was a bad idea to think of Reece as anything more than a friend, Sarah tried to focus on the conversation. "At last count, all but one action figure melted to the heating coil and the dishwasher has been out of commission ever since."

"And yet you don't look angry," he observed, his

voice warm with an amusement that was wreaking havoc with her control.

Why was this happening, she wondered as she viciously scraped at the last of the dinner dishes. Why now, of all times? Why Reece, of all people? Hadn't she gotten enough rejection when he'd kissed her and run? Or was she so masochistic that she couldn't stop herself from begging for more?

It was ridiculous. Absurd. Unbelievably awful. This was Vanessa's husband. She had no right to be looking at him. Thinking about him. *Wanting him.*

And yet she did think about him. She did want him. She couldn't seem to help herself. Her libido had been on hiatus for six long years. That it had chosen now, this moment, to wake up felt like a personal betrayal.

But she was an adult. She could control herself, no matter how hot he made her. And she was hot, her skin so sensitive that even the water sliding over her hands felt like an intimate caress.

Glancing at him sideways, she watched as his muscles rippled beneath the worn T-shirt that fit him like a glove. What she wouldn't give to be able to touch him as intimately.

Vanessa's husband, she reminded herself as she slammed the plate onto the counter and shut off the water. He was Vanessa's husband.

Grabbing a towel, she dried her hands as she headed for the family room. She had to get away from—

"Sarah?" Reece's voice stopped her in her tracks. It was even huskier than usual, lower and more sensual than she'd ever heard it. Suddenly, the shivers shooting down her spine turned to full-fledged quakes. "Where are you going?"

Her mind went blank. "I don't— Out to the family room, I guess."

"Come here." He was speaking so low now that she was sure she had imagined the words. But the expression on his face told her everything she wanted to know. More.

She should run. Just back out of the kitchen and take the stairs two at a time until she was barricaded in her bedroom out of harm's way. Oh, she knew Reece would never force her to do anything she didn't want, but that was the problem. She wanted him more than she should. More than was wise.

"I don't think that's a good idea." Was that breathy sound her voice?

"I think it's a very good idea." He put down the towel and leaned against the counter, feet crossed at the ankles. Watched her with all the intensity of a jungle cat.

"Why?"

"Because I want to hold you."

"Why now? The last time you did, you ran away like your hair was on fire."

"I was stupid."

She snorted, even as she took a cautious step back. "You're a lot of things, Reece. Stupid isn't one of them."

"Scared, then." He didn't move, but every part of him seemed to go on alert, his eyes tracking her retreat as if she was prey.

"Scared of me?"

"Scared of what you make me feel."

Her breath caught in her throat. "What do I make you feel?"

"Too much." He sighed. "More than I should feel. More than I want to feel."

"You can't say that and expect me to come to you." Her knees were weak.

"Why not?"

"You don't want me!"

"I beg to differ." He glanced down, and she realized for the first time that he was as aroused as she was.

"No." It was a cry from the battered place inside of her that had gone so long without love. "You want sex. You don't want me. You couldn't." She wrapped her arms around herself in an effort to keep from falling to sexually charged pieces.

He was across the room in a second. Then she was pressed against him—chest to chest, thigh to thigh, the proof of his desire resting hot and hard against her. "Why couldn't I?"

"Vanessa."

"Is gone."

"What's changed?" She pushed against him, but it was like pushing against a sun-warmed cliff. "You ran halfway across the country to get away from me. I'm still the same person I was then."

"But I'm not the same man."

"Of course you are."

"No. I spent most of my time in California thinking

about you. So much that the work suffered for the first time in my life." He bent his head, nibbled on her ear.

"Reece—" Her protest was weak, her resistance growing weaker.

"Hear me out, Sarah." He skimmed his lips over her jaw to her lips, where his tongue lazily traced the edge of her bottom lip.

"I've wanted you for weeks. For months—since before I moved in here. And yes, I've hated myself for it. Fought against it. But I was wrong."

"Vanessa—"

"Stop bringing her up. This is between you and me."

"Bullshit." She didn't know where she found the strength to shove at him, but she did. Satisfaction roared through her as his head snapped back in surprise. "You can tell me it's just the two of us here, but we both know that's a crock. She's here, right between us. On my side as much as on yours."

"She's only there if we put her there."

"How can we not put her there? From the day we met, she's been there. It's where she belongs."

"Vanessa's dead, Sarah."

"You think I don't know that?"

He tilted his head to the side, studied her. "I don't know that you do." He held a hand up before she could protest. "I'm not saying that to be obnoxious. I'm saying that because until I got your phone call about Rose, I didn't really, truly comprehend what it meant for Vanessa to be dead. She's not coming back and we can't live the rest of our lives like she is."

"But this thing—" She gestured helplessly between them, shocked at how quickly everything was spinning out of her control.

"You mean our attraction for one another?" He wrapped an arm around her waist and pulled her against him. This time she didn't fight him.

"Yes."

"What about it?"

"Don't you feel guilty?" She waited for his answer like her life depended on it. And maybe it did.

"Not anymore."

"Why?"

"Sarah, life is precious. We know that better than most. If we make each other happy, why shouldn't we take the happiness where we can get it? I can't imagine that Vanessa would hold it against us."

She wanted to believe him, the need to trust what he was saying—to trust him—so necessary that it was literally tearing her apart. But to do that she had to step outside of her comfort zone. To trust when suspicion came so much more naturally.

"You don't know that."

"I do know it."

"Reece—"

"Come with me to bed, Sarah. Let me hold you. It doesn't have to go any further than that."

She laughed despite the urge to cry. "Said the spider to the fly."

His smile was tender, yet so hot it rekindled the desire their argument had put a damper on.

"I need to hold you, Sarah. To feel you against me."

Part of her wanted to say no, to focus on all the reasons they shouldn't be together. But as she looked into eyes that were surprisingly open, surprisingly vulnerable, she realized he was anticipating a rejection. He'd laid himself bare, opened himself and his emotions to her, even though he was expecting her to turn away.

The bravery of the act was breathtaking when she considered how long and how hard she'd worked to protect herself. When she realized that she would never be brave enough to do what he had done.

And that's when she knew. She couldn't turn him away, couldn't walk away. Not when she needed him as desperately as he seemed to need her. Not when she wanted to hold him in the night, wanted to feel his warmth against her when the fears and insecurities and nightmares crept in.

Inch by inch, centimeter by centimeter, she leaned forward until her lips were only a hairbreadth from his. "Don't hurt me again, Reece. I don't think I could take it if you did."

"Sarah, my darling." He wrapped her in his arms, his embrace the warmest, most solid, most real thing she'd ever felt. "Don't you know that hurting you means hurting myself?"

His lips spanned the infinitesimal space between them. And any reservations she had were buried beneath the desire that shot through her like a firecracker on the Fourth of July.

CHAPTER THIRTEEN

SOMEHOW THEY MADE IT to her room. Reece didn't remember the journey, didn't remember lifting his mouth from Sarah's long enough to actually make the decision to move. He vaguely recalled bumping into some sharp piece of furniture on the way—his outer thigh still throbbed from the encounter—but everything else was a blur. An inconsequential detail next to the only fact that mattered.

Sarah was in his arms, her body pressed against his. Her mind and heart and soul open to his for the very first time.

He wanted to take it slow, to savor her, to make this moment last forever.

He wanted to throw her on the bed and take her like a wild man, to taste and take everything she had to give then demand more.

He wanted everything from her, needed it with an intensity that bordered on madness. Erotic images flashed through his mind—Sarah on the bed, naked. Waiting for him. Sarah up against the wall, crying his name as he pounded into her again and again. Sarah, lost in passion, her skin flushed a rosy pink as she gave herself up to the maelstrom of pleasure and emotion that seethed between them.

He wanted it all, wanted everything, but he was too far gone to take it. He couldn't unlock his arms from around her, couldn't let her go even for the brief moments it would take to strip her and himself.

Inhaling sharply, he fought the monstrous need clawing through him. Tried to relax, to focus so that he could bring them both pleasure. He was almost too far gone, his need to be inside her taking precedence over everything else.

"Reece?" she asked, her voice soft and trembly. "Why did you stop?"

His laugh was harsh, but he kept his voice low as he buried his head in the curve between her neck and her shoulder. He licked her and she tasted like sunshine—warm, happy, beautiful. "I'm trying to calm down. Otherwise this will be over before we get started."

It was her turn to laugh, then she moved away from him. "Oh, no. I don't think so." She pulled her red T-shirt over her head and stood there, bare from the waist up. "I've waited six years for this and I'm going to savor every second of it."

He nearly had a heart attack as he saw her unclothed for the first time, the blood rushing from his head to his groin so quickly that the room went dark around the edges. She was beautiful, amazing, her skin gleaming like alabaster in the dim light.

Her words danced through his head, and he tried to make sense of them. But it was hard when his entire focus was on her small, perfectly formed breasts. He swore his mouth began to water with the need to kiss, to suckle.

He was leaning down, intent on finding out if she tasted as good as she looked, when her words finally sank in. "Six years?" he demanded, pulling away just enough to get a clear look at her face. At her eyes. "You haven't been with anyone since Mike?"

She froze, her eyes widening as she saw his shock. "I don't sleep around, Reece."

"I never thought you did. It's just—"

"Besides, when would I have time?"

"Good point. But still—"

"I don't want to hear it, so don't say it. Don't say anything." With a grin, she popped her hand over his mouth. "I swear, I shouldn't have mentioned it. With all your gaping and gasping, you're going to give me a complex."

"I didn't mean it like that. It's just, *six years*—"

"Yes, *six years*. Now, am I going to end up going for seven or are you actually going to do something about it?"

"Of course I'm going to do something about it," he answered with a grin, his eyes sweeping over her. "I'm trying to decide where to start. I…"

His voice trailed off as he realized how sacred a gift Sarah was giving him and it humbled him, even as it made him burn hotter. Despite having three children. she was all but untouched, and her willingness to break her self-imposed celibacy for him made him tremble.

His need to satisfy her doubled, until all he could

think about was making her burn as he was. Making her scream as he wanted to. Doing anything and everything he wanted to her beautiful, vulnerable body.

Closing his eyes, Reece clenched his fists and prayed his control was as good as he thought it was.

"Do you want to stop?" The sassiness was gone from her voice and in its place was a sadness that nearly broke his heart.

"No." He didn't mean for his reply to come out quite so vehemently, but the little relieved grin she shot him told him he'd said exactly the right thing. "Really. I'm still wondering where to start."

"I thought we'd already started," she teased. "But if you need some direction—" Before he had an inkling of what she was doing, she reached forward and tugged his shirt over his head.

Leaning forward, he skimmed his mouth over her collarbone before moving onto her shoulder. "Your skin is gorgeous," he murmured, lingering at the hollow of her throat. "Like the softest satin."

She sighed, her body melting into his as he worked his way, slowly, over every exposed inch. Lust rose in him at this most visible sign of surrender, sharp, painful, inescapable. He wanted to pull her inside of him and hold her close to his heart—so close she would never be able to get away.

Because he couldn't stop himself, he plunged his hands into her short, spiky hair and pulled her against him so tightly that he could feel her hard nipples press into his chest with every rapid rise and fall of her chest.

His fingers fisted in her hair, knotting, tangling, as he fused his mouth to hers.

She tasted like paradise—warm sand, soft music and sunshine after a hard, gloomy rain. She was everything he wanted, everything he hadn't known he'd needed in these long months of sadness and pain. She *was* his sunshine and as his mouth crushed hers, his tongue plunging inside to taste and explore, he gave thanks for everything that had come before. Everything that had brought him here, to Sarah.

She was going to explode—Sarah was certain of it. Heat, furious and electric, was shooting through her body—encompassing every part of her. Leaving nothing untouched. Her lungs, her brain, her blood, her heart all were engaged. All were desperate for him.

"Reece," she murmured against his hard mouth. "I need you."

"I know, baby. I know." His hands dropped to her jeans, working the button and zipper so quickly that it felt like magic. He shoved her pants and underwear down her legs, then did the same with his own. Then backed her up until her knees met the bed and she had nowhere to go but down.

But that was fine with her—there was nowhere on earth she'd rather be at this moment than right here, in Reece's arms. Her hips lifted, hard against him as the need in her belly spiraled out of control. "I need—"

"I know." It was a curse, a prayer, a gasp for breath as his lips—his wicked, wonderful lips—raced over every part of her.

"Reece!" It was an announcement of her pleasure. A demand for the completion he dangled just out of reach.

"Sarah," he breathed back at her, right before his mouth closed over her nipple.

She would have screamed if she had enough air to do so. It was as if every vital function in her body had shut down and all she could concentrate on was the pleasure. The voluptuous pleasure that he brought to her so easily.

She was on fire, her need swamping every inhibition, every caution, every fear she'd had. Making them insignificant in the face of his passion.

With each swipe of his tongue over her nipple, each tug of his teeth, he sent her higher. Her body rocked against his, pleading for what only he could give her and still he refused. Instead he pulled her nipple into his mouth and bit her, softly but with enough of an edge that she was jackknifing up, her hands fisting in his hair.

"Do it," she gasped as she pulled him up and over her. "Do it now."

"Soon," he whispered, his grin wicked and wild and oh, so dark. "You're not ready yet."

"If I get any more ready, I'll explode."

He winked at her. "Promises, promises." He went about driving her right to the edge of sanity and beyond.

Her breath came in short gasps, and she tried to wrap her legs around him, to hold him to her, but he would have none of it. Instead he skimmed his mouth down her body, pausing to nuzzle and taste and tease from her elbow to her hip bone—and everything in between.

"Reece," she cried again, as she felt his breath against the most intimate part of her. "I need—"

"Shh, baby," he murmured as he slipped one finger inside of her. "I know. I know."

She felt his touch inside her, felt him in her deepest core and for a moment she wanted to weep. It was so perfect, so beautiful, so unbelievably right to be here like this—with him.

As he kissed her for the first time, his tongue stroking, sliding, slipping inside of her, she began to sob. It felt so good and it had been so long....

One more press of his finger deep inside of her, one more soft glide of his tongue and she was shattering— her body breaking apart and spinning wildly beyond her control. She held on to him, her fingers digging into his shoulders, her legs wrapped around his torso.

"Reece," she sobbed. "Reece, please."

"I've got you." His voice was low, tortured, his skin drawn tightly over his cheekbones as he fought for control.

"Now," she demanded, pulling him over her. Unwilling, unable, to take no for an answer. "Do it now."

Relief rocketed through her as she felt him pressing against her, hot, hard, insistent. Rising above her, he slid slowly forward, inch by inch.

"Hurry!" she demanded, wrapping her legs around him and squeezing him from the inside out.

He stopped, swore, as sweat dripped off his forehead and onto her chest. "I don't want to hurt you," he gasped. "You're so tight."

"I don't care." Her head was thrashing back and forth on the pillow, her desperation for him overwhelming everything but having him completely inside of her.

"I care." He continued to slide in and pull out, going a little deeper each time he entered her.

"Reece." She was begging, pleading. Her world was focused on this one moment, this one man. She needed him. *Needed him.* Reaching around, she grabbed his hips and pulled him down with all her might, even as she arched her hips up and against him.

"Sarah," he said hoarsely as her feminine muscles gripped him like a fist.

"Finish it," she panted. "Now."

He couldn't breathe as he paused, waited for her body to accept him when what he really wanted to do was slam into her so hard and fast that she would never forget him. He wanted to be so deep she would never get him out. *Could* never get him out.

Finally, her muscles relaxed a little—enough to let him breathe again.

She shivered with pleasure, her nails digging into his shoulders while her long, luxurious legs wrapped around his waist. And he began to move, plunging into her over and over again. Thrusting hard, going deep, driving through her as if his very life depended on it.

He felt her tighten around him, felt her orgasm take her and still he didn't stop. Kept surging into her, tilting her hips to get a better angle, riding her through one climax and well on the way to another.

Her nails scraped down his back, her breath came hot

and hard against his ear and he knew he couldn't hold on much longer. Every muscle in his body tightened until it was painful. Every nerve ending was alive and shrieking for relief. Sensation built and built, her wordless moans and gasps pushing him even higher. Higher than he'd ever gone before. Higher than he'd ever dreamed possible.

It had never been like this, like a volcano on the brink of eruption. Like a freight train on the brink of derailment. He'd never felt such a hunger to possess another person.

"Reece." It was a high-pitched, keening cry and it smashed his control.

With one final thrust, he let himself go, his release both shattering and transcendent. He took her with him, her convulsing muscles sending him even higher as the most intense orgasm of his life roared through him. He couldn't think, couldn't move—could only submit to the fiery pleasure washing through him, over her. Between them.

When it was over, when the storm had passed and it was just her and him intertwined, arms and legs wrapped around each other, he turned his head and brushed a kiss over her elbow. It was the only part of her his mouth could reach.

"I may never be able to move again." It wasn't a complaint, only the simple truth.

Sarah gave a little whimper of agreement. He was still inside her, unable to work up the strength to roll over, and she clenched her muscles around him. Sent an involuntary shiver of pleasure over his sensitized nerve endings that had him gasping and pressing a little deeper.

"I thought you couldn't move," she murmured sleepily.

"Yeah, well, being inside you seems to bring out the caveman in me."

"Thank God." She bit his shoulder, then soothed the small hurt away with her tongue.

He wanted to stay here forever, buried inside her. She was everything he'd ever wanted and nothing he thought he would ever deserve. He'd never felt luckier—or more unworthy.

Stroking his fingers down her arm, he cracked his eyes open a little bit—enough to study her. She looked a picture—her lips swollen from his kisses, her white skin flushed a rosy, inviting pink. Her arms were sprawled to the side, her breasts thrust upward, her nipples still hard from his attentions.

How had he gone this long without her? How had he spent his life without ever knowing this kind of passion existed?

For a moment, thoughts of Vanessa pushed at him, but he blocked them out. This wasn't the time or the place. Now was for Sarah, for him. For the two of them. There would be time enough later to worry about all the complications that made up their lives. For now, he wanted to lie here and revel in the simple perfection that was making love to Sarah.

She seemed to feel the same way and for long

minutes they drifted, their bodies limp with completion, loose with satiation. But was he really satisfied, he wondered, as he stroked a finger down her breast and watched her nipple peak prettily. He couldn't stop touching her, didn't want to stop. He wanted to explore every inch of Sarah, to taste every part of her from her forehead to her toes. And then he wanted to start all over again, until there was no part of her he hadn't claimed.

Rolling to his back with great effort, he gathered her against him. Then reached down and brought her hand to his mouth. He used his lips to tickle her fingers, pulled one into his mouth and curled his tongue around it, reveling in the hitch in her breathing, the sudden increase in the pulse that beat so steadily beneath his hand.

Relinquishing the first finger, he pulled the second into his mouth and did the same thing. Over and over until he'd tasted every finger and was more than half-crazed with the need to have her again.

"Can you take me again?" he asked, his body jerking violently against hers as it searched for satisfaction.

"Yes," she murmured, wrapping her arms around him and tugging until he was once again on top of her. "I'll always take you."

Her words touched him like nothing ever had, sending him careening over an invisible ledge he hadn't known he was close to. As he thrust inside of her again—taking her more slowly and gently this time—he realized that there would be no more walking away. No more hiding. He loved Sarah, with a passion and intensity he hadn't thought possible.

He didn't know when it had happened, nor did he understand why it had occurred with everything—good and bad—that was between them. All he knew was that he loved her and he wasn't letting her go. Not when he had the chance to keep her forever.

The thought had him coming, his body releasing in great spasms and dragging Sarah along with it. No, there was no escape for her. She just didn't know it yet.

CHAPTER FOURTEEN

"MOMMY, WAKE UP! It's Saturday. No school. No school! It's time to go to the park. Wake up."

Sarah came to consciousness slowly, from a sleep so deep and restful that her body felt refreshed for the first time in recent history. But then, good sex could do that to a girl. She almost snorted—*good* didn't even come close to describing what she and Reece had shared during the night.

Over and over again he'd reached for her, until she had been unable to tell where she left off and he began. For a woman who hadn't had sex in over six years, it had been an amazing feeling. For a woman who didn't know how to trust, it had been at times both frightening and exhilarating as hell.

"Mommy!" Johnny's voice wailed in her ear, right before little fingers began trying to pry her eyes open.

"Ouch!" Slapping a finger to her smarting eye, Sarah rolled over on top of Johnny and gave him a big, slobbery kiss. "Was that really necessary?"

"Yes," he giggled. "You weren't getting up."

"Well, I'm up now," she said in her scariest voice. "And hungry enough to eat two little boys." Burrowing her face into Johnny's tummy, she made noisy, slurp sounds that had both boys laughing hysterically.

"My turn, Mommy! My turn." Justin called from his spot next to the bed.

She turned to him, an expression of astonishment on her face. "Are you actually volunteering to get eaten?"

"Uh-huh!" He nodded, his little face eager and her heart literally melted with love for him.

"All right, then. You asked for it." Pulling him on top of her, she pretended to eat his bare little toes.

"Mmm-mmm. These are good. How many of them do you have, anyway?"

"Ten," he giggled.

"Ten?" She widened her eyes. "That's a lot of toes— I'd better get busy." She made more slurpy noises as she went back to devouring his toes.

"I have ten toes, too, Mommy." Johnny jumped up and down on the bed next to her, trying to shove his foot in front of his brother's. "Eat my toes! Eat my toes!"

"I think you should go for it. And if you're still hungry after all of those, I think we've got a few toes over here we can volunteer, too. Don't we, Rosie?"

Sarah stopped in midnibble, her heart racing at Reece's appearance. She felt her cheeks heat as she wondered how she should respond to him. It's not like she had much experience with mornings after.

Glancing up through her lashes, she saw Reece leaning negligently against her door frame, Rose in one hand and a cup of coffee in the other.

"I thought you might need this," he murmured, walking slowly into the room, coffee cup extended. "You didn't get much sleep last night."

Taking the cup, she sipped at the hot liquid like it was ambrosia, relishing the instant caffeine kick to her system. "Mmm," she said. "Thanks."

"No problem."

"So are you awake now, Mommy?" Justin asked, his face furrowed in a look of painful concentration.

"I do believe I am," she answered as she took another sip, careful to focus on her sons. Reece might have given her the best night of her life, but she wasn't sure she was ready to face him quite yet in the cold light of day.

"Awesome!" yelled Johnny, punching the air for emphasis. "Uncle Reece said we could go to the park and feed the ducks. He said they're always hungry on Saturday mornings."

"He did, huh?"

"Yep. But we have to go before it gets too hot. We don't want Rosie to get over—over—"

"Overheated." Justin finished his brother's sentence with a grin.

"So get up," Johnny said in a singsongy voice. "Get up, get up, get up!"

Sarah had started to throw the covers back and do just that when she realized she hadn't put on her nightgown after Reece's last bout of lovemaking. Freezing in place, she stared at the boys and wondered frantically how to get them out of the room. She really wasn't up to answering the *why are you naked, Mommy* question— especially not with Reece standing right there.

He must have sensed her dilemma, though, because after dumping Rose in front of the baby gym Sarah kept in the corner for her, he began herding the boys toward the bedroom door. "I'll tell you what. Why don't you guys get dressed then head downstairs. I've got breakfast on the table. That way your mom has a couple of minutes to enjoy her coffee and get herself dressed."

"And then we'll feed the ducks?" Johnny questioned, pausing on the threshold, his face very serious.

"And then we'll feed the ducks," Reece answered firmly. "I promise."

"I bet I can beat you!" Johnny said to his brother with a grin before taking off down the hall to his room.

"No way!" Justin chased after him, laughing. A few seconds later their bedroom door slammed closed, followed by a series of high-pitched giggles.

"Thanks for that," Sarah murmured shyly, unable to avoid looking at Reece for one second longer.

"No problem." He flopped on the bed next to her, and fingered a few strands of her hair. "But I have to admit, I had ulterior motives."

"And what are those?" she asked, her breath catching in her throat at his nearness.

This morning wasn't going at all how she'd expected it to. It was so much easier, the guilt at sleeping with Vanessa's husband not nearly as bad as she had thought it would be.

Then again, sometime in the middle of the night she'd given up thinking of Reece as Vanessa's husband

and had begun thinking of him as *her* lover. The things he could make her feel weren't friendlike in the least.

She didn't know if the carefree feeling would last— was pretty sure that it wouldn't—but for now she was going to take this chance at happiness.

"Guess." Leaning over, Reece captured her mouth in a kiss that reminded her exactly why her body was so fantastically sore this morning.

"You taste amazing," he muttered, against her lips, his tongue gently stroking the corners of her mouth.

"I taste like coffee and morning breath."

"You taste like sunshine."

She shot him an amused glance. "Have you been drinking this morning?"

He arched an eyebrow. "Should I be offended?"

"I don't know. But you're entirely too happy for someone who got—" she glanced at the clock "—about four hours of sleep."

"More like two. I let you sleep in." He stole another kiss, his hand coming up to cop a feel beneath the sheet. "I should get rewarded for that."

"Oh, really? And exactly what reward would you like?"

"I don't know, but I bet I can think of something." He stroked her nipple and she found herself arching against him.

"I bet you can." Relishing the feel of him so close to her, Sarah closed her eyes and leaned against him for a second. He was so strong that he made her feel safe and protected whenever she was in his arms. As she'd been tackling problems head-on her entire life, it was an unusual feeling. And one that she was deathly afraid she could get used to.

But that would be stupid, she reminded herself as Reece rubbed her neck and shoulders. Whatever this thing was between them, it wouldn't last forever. She had to remember that, had to stay focused. Or when he walked away, he'd take whatever was left of her heart with him.

It was a frightening thought.

Pulling away from his fabulously talented hands, she took the sheet with her as she headed toward the bathroom. "We'd better get going. The boys will be back any minute. And Rosie won't stay happy down there much longer." She glanced at her daughter to make sure she was still okay, then smiled as she watched Rose bat at the light-up balls and animals hanging from the gym.

"She's doing really well," Reece commented as he, too, studied their daughter.

"I know. The cough is just about gone and she's back to being her regular self."

"So, um, Sarah…"

She looked at Reece—really looked at him, for the first time since he'd come in the room. The uncertainty on his face had her warming like nothing else could have—he was as unsteady in this situation as she was. Maybe even more.

That realization gave her strength and a confidence she hadn't even known she was lacking. Cocking her head to the side, she smiled. "So, do you want to take a quick shower with me?"

He jumped off the bed and scooped Rose from her play mat before depositing her in the playpen. "I thought you'd never ask."

AFTER A QUICK SHOWER that was as much about water sports as it was about getting clean, Reece followed Sarah down to the kitchen, where he packed a picnic lunch while she grabbed a quick bowl of cereal.

He couldn't believe how excited he was—like a little boy with his first bike on Christmas morning, he couldn't wait to take his and Sarah's brand-new relationship for a spin.

Nothing in his life had felt as good as sinking into Sarah's arms—and body. Nothing had ever felt as right. Not even being with Vanessa, who he had loved very much, but who had always left the lovemaking in their relationship up to him—unless of course, it was her fertile time. Then she'd all but thrown him on the bed and attacked him.

After sliding the sandwiches he'd been making into Sarah's picnic basket, he reached into the fridge and pulled out a bowl of grapes. He bagged a few big bunches as he reflected on the many ways being with Sarah was different from being with Vanessa.

For one thing, Sarah gave as good as she got. Through the long night, she'd reached for him almost as often as he'd reached for her and while her lovemaking had been a lot of things, passive hadn't been one of them.

Though the old guilt rose up, he pushed it down. Refused to let it have any part of this perfect morning. For too long his and Vanessa's sex life had felt more like going through the motions than an actual means to express their love.

She'd only wanted him when she was ovulating—the rest of the time, she'd had absolutely no interest in having sex with him. And even when they were having sex, she hadn't been interested in giving or receiving pleasure so much as making sure she was in the most fertile position.

He'd gone along with her, wanting to give her what she craved, but by the end he'd lost almost all interest in having sex himself. What had been the use, when it was no longer about giving and receiving pleasure? When it was only about making a baby he hadn't even been sure that he wanted?

But with Sarah, everything was different. She wanted *him*. She wanted the physical and emotional closeness that came from making love.

"Hey, what are you thinking about?" Sarah's warm arms slipped around his waist as she rested her cheek between his shoulder blades. "You're looking awfully serious over here."

"I was thinking about you."

"Oh, really?" Her arms tightened. "Do tell."

Turning, he wrapped his arms around her and savored the feeling of having her strong, soft body resting against his. "Nothing specific, really. I was thinking about how amazing it was to be inside of you."

Her cheeks turned pink, even as her eyes shone with a pleased surprise. "Really? Because I was thinking about how amazing it was to have you inside of me."

Warmth spread through him at her words, until he only wanted to yank her back up the stairs. His body was as ready and willing as if it hadn't just spent the night being satisfied in every conceivable way.

"Mom, Uncle Reece, are you ready to go?" Johnny bounded into the kitchen with Justin hot on his heels.

Sarah's reaction was instantaneous—she jerked away from him like a scalded cat and pretended to be really interested in feeding Rose the applesauce the baby had rejected ten minutes before.

Even as he told himself that, of course, they should keep what was between them private for a while—until they could figure it out—he was smarting over the distance she'd put between them. He'd waited a long time to feel this way about a woman—to explore these feelings about Sarah—and no matter how logical her reaction was, it grated that she wanted to keep things between them under wraps.

"I think so," he answered, sliding a few of Sarah's homemade cookies into the basket, along with a collection of water and juice packs while he tried his damnedest not to pout.

Then Sarah was there, next to him, as if she understood exactly what he was feeling. Putting her hand on his shoulder, she just looked at him, her blue eyes filled with understanding and affection she didn't even try to hide.

And suddenly keeping their feelings to themselves didn't seem so bad—almost as if it was a secret the two of them shared. Of course, it wasn't time for the boys to know about what was between them. He and Sarah hadn't even figured out what they had.

But as he looked into Sarah's eyes, he knew that he wanted a hell of a lot more than he'd thought possible when he'd moved in here three months before. In fact, he just might want everything.

CHAPTER FIFTEEN

"ARE YOU KIDDING ME, MATT?" Reece whispered fiercely into his cell phone as he let himself out of Sarah's room at five o'clock in the morning—as he had every morning for the past three weeks. The kids hadn't begun to stir, but he knew it was only a matter of time and he and Sarah were still keeping the physical aspect of their relationship as quiet as possible.

"I know things are crazy there with Rose and Sarah and the boys. I can't go, Reece. I wish I could, but they want you. You're the one who drew up the plans and you're the one they want to blame. I'm telling you, these guys are talking lawsuits."

"Lawsuits? What the hell for?" He continued whispering until he made his way into his bedroom and shut the door. Then it took every ounce of self-control he had not to yell.

"The CE team they hired have run into a bunch of problems—they're saying you did a crap job on the plans."

"Damn civil engineers—half the time they don't know what the hell to do with plans when they get them. There was nothing wrong with those plans, Matt. I went over them dozens of times."

"I know. But this was the project you were working on when Vanessa died. Do you think, maybe—"

"No. The plans were solid—better than solid. They were fantastic and you know it."

"That's what I thought, but I had to ask."

Reece sighed, then ran a hand through his hair in a gesture of pure, out-and-out frustration. "Look, I'll stop by the office, download the files and send them to you. You can see for yourself the mistakes weren't on our end."

"That's great." Matt's voice was overly solicitous, as if speaking to someone he expected to lose it at any second. "But you still need to go, Reece. There's no choice."

Reece knew that. Just as he knew the trip was going to totally screw him up with Sarah. "Why now? Things are complicated as hell here and this is the worst possible time."

"Murphy's law, man."

Wasn't that the truth, Reece reflected as he hung up the phone after promising Matt he'd be on a flight out the next morning. They rarely had problems like this and usually their out-of-town travel was limited to a few days here or there.

But if Matt was right and the CEs had messed this up, it would take a lot more than a few days to get things turned around. Which meant leaving Rose and the boys again, even though he'd only been home a month. It meant leaving Sarah again. And just the thought made him feel like a total heel.

How was he supposed to get her to believe him when

he said he cared about her? Now that he'd made love to her—and wanted to stick around—he was bound for Hawaii for weeks.

He'd have to be sure she understood that he wasn't running away. Because, honestly, he couldn't imagine living the rest of his life without her.

Wandering down to the kitchen, he started the coffee, knowing that Sarah would be down soon. It was a time both of them had begun to treasure—these early-morning talks over coffee, while the house was still quiet around them. It was a chance for them to talk without interruptions, to savor the joy they felt in being together.

But not today. He had no desire to tell Sarah he was leaving, any more than he knew she'd want to hear it. It wasn't like he had a choice, though.

The coffee had barely finished dripping, when Sarah bounded into the kitchen, all rosy and warm from bed. He watched as she poured them both coffee, adding a packet of sweetener to hers and a splash of milk to his.

How stupid was he that that little flash of domesticity, that little proof that she knew him and cared about his likes and dislikes, filled him with an overwhelming warmth?

He crossed the kitchen in a flash, had his lips on Sarah's before she could get the milk back in the fridge.

"Mmm, well, good morning," she murmured, her body going soft and pliant against his. "Maybe we should head back upstairs. The kids won't be up for another half an hour."

He was tempted to take her up on the offer, but his imminent departure was hanging over his head, making him feel guilty as hell, even though he knew he was doing nothing wrong.

Because he'd rather get it over with, he took a deep breath and blurted, "I have to leave tomorrow, Sarah." He said the words quickly, as they left a bad taste in his mouth. "There's a problem in Hawaii that I can't get out of. I've tried, but things are exploding there."

SARAH'S WORLD tilted on its axis, and for a minute all she heard was that Reece was leaving. But after a few seconds the rest of his words sank in and she tried to be reasonable, to tell herself that this wasn't the same as last time. "I understand work commitments, Reece. I told you that before."

"We both know that I didn't go to California for work. Or at least not exclusively for work."

Her heart was beating too fast, and her breathing was uneven. "This time—"

"This time it is exclusively for work. And if Matt wasn't tied up in California, and the customer wasn't demanding that I be there, I wouldn't be going." He shrugged, looking as unhappy as she felt. "I'm not ready to leave you, not by a long shot. But Matt can't do it and someone needs to be there."

"Okay." She eased out of his embrace, backed away with studied nonchalance even while she was shaking apart on the inside. She didn't want to hear this, didn't want to know this—not now, not after the past few weeks. He was making too many excuses, and looking far too uncomfortable for this to be the whole truth. "Reece—"

"I swear, Sarah, it's not like last time."

"I told you, it's fine." But it wasn't fine and they both knew it. With each word he said, each excuse he gave, her past was coming back to her. Her father's words, pounding in her head. Mike's words doing the same.

"No, it isn't." He crossed the room and tried to pull her into his arms, but she stepped back, refusing to be placated with sex. "I'm leaving you holding the bag— again. If there was any other way—"

"I've been holding the bag my whole life, Reece. A couple weeks here or there is no big deal."

"That's not what I meant."

"I know what you meant." Forcing a smile, she leaned over and kissed his cheek. "Do you mind listening for Rosie while I take a quick shower? It's going to be a busy day."

"Of course. But I wasn't finished yet. I am sorry—"

"And I told you there's nothing to be sorry for. Work is work. I get it. Now, I bought Rose a whole slew of new outfits yesterday. Go pick out a pretty one for her."

With that, she ran up the stairs and into the bathroom to turn the shower on, then brushed her teeth while waiting for the water to heat up. She opened a new bottle of shower gel and filed her nails. Did any and everything she could come up with to avoid thinking of the conversation she and Reece had just had.

But when she was in the shower, the hot water beating

down on her, she couldn't avoid the pain any longer. Tears she refused to shed burned in her eyes, even as she told herself she was being stupid.

Why was she taking this so hard? She'd known all along that he wasn't going to stick around, had known after their kiss that he was running away from what they felt for each other. Why should this morning have been any different?

Because, he'd taken everything from her. No, she told herself, trying to be as honest as possible. She'd given everything to him, even knowing that to do so was a risk. But she had wanted him, had needed him. Had trusted him.

Even knowing how much she had to lose, she had trusted him. So why was she complaining when that trust had backfired? Hadn't her whole life been one long string of misplaced trust? Why should Reece be any different?

But he had been different, she admitted, as she searched inside herself and realized that he had shattered some vulnerable place inside her she hadn't even known existed. Had pulled her kicking and screaming back to life.

All along she'd been harboring hope that things might really work out between them, no matter what defenses she put up. All along, she'd been praying that he wasn't like her father. Wasn't like her mother. Wasn't like her husband. All along, she'd been hoping that he wouldn't run when things got tough.

She should have known better. After all, he'd run twice before—after Vanessa had died and after he'd kissed her. At the first show of opposition, at the first thing that made him the least bit uncomfortable, Reece had been out the door so fast it was amazing he hadn't tripped over his own feet.

Why had she expected this time to be different? Just because he'd stuck around a few weeks didn't mean he had any intention of sticking for the long haul.

Her laugh was low and bitter, even as she scrubbed at her body with an intensity she knew would leave marks. She wanted to erase his touch, wanted to scrub his delicious, masculine scent off her body so that it wouldn't hurt so much.

Calm down. It doesn't matter. You're both the same people you were yesterday, the same people you'll be tomorrow. And she knew that was true, had learned that lesson when Mike had lit out.

But it hadn't hurt this much when Mike had left, hadn't felt like she was being ripped in half. Maybe because by the time he left, she'd been almost glad to see him go. Or maybe, it was because—even from the beginning—she'd known he wasn't the type to stick around.

But Reece, Reece had stuck around for Vanessa. He'd dealt with her losing her job, losing her mother. Had been right beside her through the infertility treatments and her nearly crazed desire to have a baby. He hadn't had to travel constantly. Hell, he hadn't gone anywhere at all. Not like now.

So it had to be her, then. He simply didn't feel for her the way he'd felt for Vanessa.

But he'd come back to Sarah the last time. He hadn't been able to stay away.

But he'd returned for Rose, a little voice whispered in her head. He'd had no intention of coming back to her until Rose had gotten sick. He'd told her a few days earlier, that he might have to be in California for a couple more weeks at the minimum.

And it had been a lie. Everything had been a lie. He'd been out there to get away from her, to get away from the feelings she had for him.

Part of her wanted to rush out of the shower and confront Reece. To demand an answer to the questions that burned inside of her.

Why was he so different with her than he'd been with Vanessa? What was it about her that brought out the worst in the men in her life? Was she really that unlovable? Really so not worth sticking around for once things got tough?

What was wrong with her?

But she couldn't do that. Refused to do it. He wanted her to understand, to believe the story about Hawaii like he'd expected her to swallow the one about California. And while it grated on her pride that he thought she was so stupid, at the same time she was determined not to let him see how much he'd hurt her.

She could fake it for a day, act like everything was

normal. Send him off with a hug and directions to be safe. Then spend the time he was gone shoring up her defenses so that he could never slip through again.

SOMETHING WAS WRONG with Sarah. Reece watched her covertly as she slid the lasagna out of the oven and onto the kitchen table. They'd been together all day—taking the kids to the park then out for pizza and to the mall for some winter clothes for the boys, as the days were finally getting cooler.

Even after they'd gotten home, he and Sarah had hung out together, watching TV, cooking dinner, playing with the kids. She'd been with him every step of the way, laughing, playing, talking. Yet she'd never seemed farther away.

He'd tried to talk to her after he'd gotten Rosie to sleep, but she'd rushed off to play pirates with the boys. He'd cornered her in the kitchen, but she'd merely laughed and kissed him until he forgot his name let alone whatever it had been he wanted to ask her.

But even her kisses had been different than usual— still hot and mind-numbing, but it was as if she'd turned a part of herself off. As if that special part of her that made her Sarah was missing.

With a sigh, he slid Rosie into her high chair and started to feed her the mashed carrots and applesauce that Sarah had set out. Part of him wanted to confront her right now—to say to hell with everything else until they got settled whatever it was that had her so upset.

But he was adult enough to realize that this wasn't

the time—not with the kids awake and still hyped up from their "super-duper day," as Justin had taken to calling it. So Reece kept his mouth shut as he fed Rosie. Bit his tongue while he helped Sarah clean up after dinner. And gritted his teeth through the endlessly long ritual of getting the boys settled for the night while Sarah fed the baby.

When the kids were finally asleep and the house was quiet, he went in search of Sarah. He started in Rosie's room, but the baby was sound asleep in her crib, her mother nowhere to be found.

He could feel his own anger building as he hunted, checking first downstairs then heading back upstairs to her bedroom. Was it hypocritical of him to be this upset at Sarah for retreating after they'd made love, when he had done much the same thing after their first explosive kiss?

Perhaps, but after a long day of trying to talk to her, he wasn't inclined to make excuses for her behavior—or his own. He just wanted to have it out so that he could have the sweet, sexy woman he'd come to know in his arms.

Why couldn't she yell and shout? This sulking and holding things to herself was enough to drive a man insane, especially one who was desperate to figure out what was going on in her head.

He found Sarah in her bedroom, sitting in front of her makeup table, spinning a ring between her fingers. There was so much he wanted to say to her, so many questions he wanted to ask.

Keeping his smile in place and a rein on his temper,

he started with the inane. "What is that?" He nodded to the ring.

It took her so long to answer that he started thinking she was deliberately ignoring him. But finally she said, her voice low and subdued, "My wedding band."

It wasn't the answer he'd been expecting and it hit him in the gut, ripping out his stomach and heart with one fatal blow. Shock—and fear—carried him across the room. Was she regretting sleeping with him because he wasn't her husband? Was she upset that she'd given in to the overwhelming heat between them?

He didn't know how to ask, didn't have a clue what to say. But she wasn't talking and unless he wanted to leave, he had to think of something.

"Do you still love him?" He tried to keep his voice gentle even as he wanted to howl in outrage. How could she love that bastard? He'd married her, gotten her pregnant then abandoned her before the twins were even born. Mike was a selfish ass—

Reece froze as the parallels slowly hit him. Hadn't he done the same thing to her? Gotten Sarah pregnant— albeit not in the conventional sense—and then left her, pregnant and alone because he couldn't deal?

Shame ate at him, silencing the burn of anger that had kept him going for most of the afternoon. As he got out of his head, he realized Sarah hadn't answered him. Hadn't responded to the question at all.

"You don't have to answer that."

She glanced over her shoulder at him, smiling that same damn wrong smile that had driven him crazy all afternoon. "I hadn't planned on it."

"Can you at least tell me what's wrong?" He crossed the room and crouched down next to her so that they were eye to eye. "You've been acting strangely all day."

"Noth—"

"Don't say nothing, damn it," he exploded, the anger closer to the surface than he'd thought. "I know something's upset you."

Sarah tossed her head back and stood, fury in every line of her body. "Don't you dare come into my bedroom and order me around. Do I chase you down and demand that you tell me everything going on in your head?"

"That's different." Even as he said it, the words sounded lame to him.

"Oh, really? You want to tell me exactly why it's different?"

"You're shutting me out, Sarah, and it's driving me crazy."

She laughed, but it was a bitter, twisted sound. "You were never in, Reece. It's hard to shut you out of something I never gave you access to."

Anger flared, but he tamped it down. Now wasn't the time, not when Sarah was hurting. And she *was* hurting, even if she wasn't willing to admit it to him.

He wrapped his hands around her wrists. "Sarah, baby—"

"Let it go, Reece." She shook her head. "It's been a strange day and I'm feeling a little off."

He wanted to push, to break through the barriers she'd erected between them, but he was smart enough to know that wouldn't help his cause. Perhaps if he eased it out of her…

"Do you want me to leave?"

Hurt flashed in her eyes, even as they widened. "The house?"

"I meant your room, but of course, you've got the other alternative."

"You're being ridiculous, Reece."

"Am I?" He nudged her close, shutting his eyes at the feel of her body pressed so intimately against his own. "I want to be with you, Sarah."

She pulled back, stared into his eyes for what felt like an eternity. "Do you?"

"More than I want my next breath."

"Then stay." The words were wrenched from her, but the eyes staring back at him were solid. Resolute. "Make love to me."

For long seconds they stayed where they were, eyes locked, hearts beating in the same rhythm. Finally, when he could take no more of the sexual tension stretching so tightly between them, he trailed one finger down her bare forearm.

Sarah was his and tonight he would claim her so well and so powerfully that when the morning came and he had to leave, there would be no misunderstanding about who she belonged to. Mike and his damn ring could go to hell.

Goose bumps rose wherever Reece touched, then spread to encompass Sarah's whole body. She shivered violently and he asked, "Are you cold?" But Sarah could see his grin, knew that Reece was aware of what was making her shudder.

Maybe she was being stupid to do this. Maybe she

was asking for heartbreak. But as she'd gone through the day with him and seen his genuine joy in Rose and Justin and Johnny, she had begun to question her interpretations of his motives.

He hadn't acted like a man caught in the grip of debilitating guilt. He had laughed and teased and played with the kids until they were completely worn-out. And he had treated her like a lover—stealing kisses whenever the kids' attention was directed elsewhere. Touching her intimately, whispering sweet and sexy things in her ears. In short, behaving like a man who was perfectly content where he was.

So, somewhere along the way, she'd decided to give him the benefit of the doubt. To trust him—if not with her soul, then at least with her very fragile heart. If her trust proved misguided, then she would be the only one to suffer. But if it wasn't—that thought was the most tantalizing of all. If her trust was justified, her whole world would be a better place.

"Sarah?" Reece's voice was low, a gravelly whisper that sent shivers of arousal down her spine. "Where'd you go?"

She shook her head. "I'm right here."

They were standing so close that his breath had become hers, his heartbeat pulsing in perfect rhythm to her own. She took a moment to revel in the intimacy of being this close to him before giving in to the demand that was thrumming through her body.

Her body was on fire, the need she had for him growing with every second. Besides, she was sure—

now that she knew to be wary—that she could handle it. Could stop herself from giving him everything.

Tilting her head, she relished the feel of his warm breath against her neck. She might not be willing to give him her soul, but she could give him her body. And take his in return—tonight and for as long as she had him.

"Kiss me," she murmured, sliding her hands up his chest to link behind his neck.

His grin was almost feral. "With pleasure."

Then his mouth was on hers and she forgot that he was leaving tomorrow, forgot all the excuses she'd given herself as she lay awake nights wanting him. And let herself feel. Just feel.

He pulled her closer, so that the softness of her breasts pressed against the hard muscles of his chest. Her nipples ached and she rubbed against him desperate for relief. His fingers fisted in her hair, tilting her head back so that his mouth fused tightly to hers.

He devoured her—there was no other word for it— and she let him. Welcomed him. His hands tugged harshly on her hair while his mouth crushed hers with a wild abandon that excited her almost beyond bearing. She wanted more, needed more.

Slipping her hands between them, she tore at his shirt—heedless of the buttons that scattered. He laughed wickedly and shrugged out of the shirt.

"Is this what you want?" he asked as he went to work on her buttons. Within moments he had divested her of her blouse and bra and they were skin to skin. She gasped with the exquisite relief of it.

"Not yet," she answered, breathlessly, her hands moving restlessly over his chest and shoulders. Relishing the hard planes and muscles that were so different than her own softness. "But soon."

He groaned, then slid his hands up to cup her face. Easing away, he slowed things down for a moment. "You are so beautiful." His voice was soft, reverent, and she felt her heart tremble in her chest. She tried to ignore it, to force her emotions back, but she couldn't do it. Not now, not with Reece. No matter how much it would hurt later on.

"So are you." Following his rhythm, she let her fingertips trail lightly over his nipples and down his flat stomach. She found the small line of hair that started below his belly button and began to stroke it, letting her fingers delve past his belt buckle a little more with each sweeping pass.

He leaned down and crushed her mouth with his. Claimed her—with his tongue and teeth and terrible hunger. And she relished the feel of him, the light, citrusy taste of him so at odds with the dangerous need she could feel building between them.

His hands cupped her breasts and he bent his head to take one hard nipple into his mouth. She bucked against him, moaning even as she arched to give him better access.

"More," she demanded, her hands tangling in his hair as her womb contracted tightly. Emptily.

"Soon," he said, lifting his head and moving to her other breast and suckling her.

She went wild, her body rocking against his. She was warm and wet and empty—so empty. All she wanted was for him to fill her, to take the chill away. But he was taking a wicked delight in tormenting her.

Reaching down, she fumbled with his belt buckle, her fingers suddenly unable to perform the simplest of tasks. "Take them off," she demanded and he chuckled hotly.

Thrusting her away from him, Reece stripped his pants off then did the same for her. He was deliberately rough, deliberately harsh, and the excitement spiraling between them spun out of control.

Sarah ran her fingers down his hard length, and he shuddered, staring at her from under half-closed lids. Sarah wasn't sure what she found more arousing—the hot, silkiness beneath her fingers or the look of barely leashed desire on his face. All she knew was that if he didn't take her soon she would spontaneously combust, right here in the middle of her bedroom.

As if he could read her thoughts, he pressed his fully aroused body against hers and walked her backward until they bumped against her bed. Grinding her hips against his, she encouraged him, and he groaned as her wetness glided over him. Then pressed more fully against her as he cupped her breasts in his hands and stroked her nipples with his thumb.

Sarah cried out—she couldn't help herself—and he bent to muffle the cry with his mouth. She was playing a dangerous game and she knew it, but was helpless to stop it in the face of her great need for him. Tomorrow would come, leaving her heartbroken and in pieces, but wasn't that better than the cold shell she had surrounded herself with these past years. Feeling something, anything, was better than the numbness that had hung around for far too long.

Lack of feeling wasn't a problem with Reece—with every stroke of his hand waves of sensation rippled through her until she was nearly incoherent with desire. "More," she demanded, grabbing his face in her hands and pulling his mouth to hers for a hot, hungry kiss that was all sharp teeth and insistent lust. "I want everything."

"Yes." His eyes were hard, his mouth grim as he gave in to the passion that flared between them. Spinning her around, he lay down on the bed and slowly brought her to rest above him.

She gasped as he entered her. Then he moved and she lost the ability to do anything but feel. Leaning forward, he nibbled her chin and throat before trailing his lips down to nip at the underside of her breast. Panting, nearly sobbing with need, she rose and fell so that he drove even more deeply inside of her.

"Yes, baby. That's it," he said, his hips surging forward to meet her. Her eyes drifted shut and he growled low in his throat, his fingers lifting to clamp on her chin. Their eyes met, locked, and he smiled grimly. "Look at me," he murmured, the melted chocolate of his eyes nearly electric with passion. "I want you to see me when I take you." He emphasized his words with a hard thrust that made her see stars.

And then he was moving—thrusting and withdrawing so slowly that she thought she would lose what little mind she had left. She tried to hurry him up, but his hands held her hips in an iron grip as he controlled the easy—excruciating—pace of their lovemaking.

Nothing existed for her but him and this moment and the lush, amazing feelings he was evoking inside of her. She wanted to linger over him so that she could feel like this forever. She wanted to race to completion, her body starving for orgasm. But she could do neither as she was caught by him, totally at his mercy.

"Reece," she whimpered, when she could take no more. "Please."

Slipping a hand between them, he stroked her and that easily she came—her body spinning wildly out of her control as spasm after spasm ripped through her. Moments later he joined her, his harsh groan mingling with the soft cries she couldn't hold back.

A long time later, as she listened to Reece's heavy breathing beside her, Sarah battled tears. Reece had given her the most beautiful sexual experience of her life, yet she'd never felt so lost. Every part of her felt empty. She'd given Reece everything she had to give, had poured every part of herself into him despite her need to hold back. And now, as the long night stretched ahead, she was left with one question. Was it enough to keep him with her?

CHAPTER SIXTEEN

"SO, HAVE YOU HEARD from Reece lately?" Tad called from the couch where he was eating potato chips and watching Monday Night Football. Pamela had gone out of town on a business trip and Sarah had invited him over for dinner to save her happy-go-lucky brother from the debacle of his own cooking.

And to keep herself from brooding, but that was another story altogether.

"Last night." She didn't pause in mixing up the batch of brownies she had promised the twins for dessert.

"How long's he been gone now?" Tad's voice came from right over her shoulder and Sarah jumped, splashing chocolate batter all over the counter and herself.

"Geez, sis, you're kind of jumpy." Tad grinned as he dipped one massive finger in the bowl for a taste.

She continued what she was doing, ignoring him easily. It was only after she'd poured the batter into a greased pan and popped that pan into the oven that she realized he was still standing behind her, silently waiting.

"Is there something you need?" she asked.

"You didn't answer me."

"About what?" She feigned an ignorance she really wished she felt.

"About Reece." His blue eyes—so similar to her own—stared at her with a mixture of amusement and concern. "How long, sis?"

"Almost three weeks." She winced at the look on his face, but didn't say a word. What could she say? Tad had been there when their father had walked out. He'd seen her after Mike had left. Was it any wonder he seemed more than a little wary of her feelings for Reece?

"I'm fine, by the way," she said, faking bravado.

His answering snort told her she hadn't been nearly as convincing as she'd hoped. "Is he coming back?"

Trust Tad to cut right to the chase. "Is that any of your business?"

"Seeing as how I have to chase him down and beat the crap out of him if he doesn't come back, yeah, I think it is my business."

Her bruised heart warmed at his words. It was nice to know that there were still some dependable men in the world. They might be few and far between, but at least they existed. "No one's beating up anyone."

"Wanna bet?" He used one of the boys' favorite phrases.

"Yes." The look she shot him was pure big sister. "Besides, there's nothing to beat him up for. He's working."

"That's what they all say."

"Leave it alone, Tad."

"Why should I? The jerk abandons you when you're

pregnant, then moves into your house without so much as an explanation. And then he runs all over the country whenever things get a little boring."

"He has to make a living."

"In Hawaii?"

"Yes, in Hawaii. And in San Francisco and wherever else his buildings are going up. He's the architect and if there are problems, he's the one who has to go fix them."

"Why are you making excuses for him?"

"Why are you jumping all over him?"

"Oh, man." Tad shook his head in disbelief.

"What?"

"I've seen this before."

"Seen what?" She couldn't keep the defensive note out of her voice.

"This single-minded preoccupation with a loser. You did it after Dad left—made excuse after excuse. With Mike, too."

"I'm not making excuses."

"You're in love with him."

Tad's pronouncement came down with all the impact of a lightning bolt, shutting her up and shaking the very foundations she'd built her life on since her sons were born.

"That's not true!" she exclaimed, but her voice was weaker than she'd heard it in a long time.

Tad studied her. "Yes, it is. Sarah, I swear, when it comes to your personal life you're a train wreck waiting to happen."

"That's—"

"What do you think is going to happen with Reece? You think he's going to fall in love with you? Marry you? The guy lost his wife and, though he may be showing an interest in you, I'm telling you it's purely sexual."

Sarah stared at her brother in wounded silence. Even though she knew he was trying to help, it still hurt to hear her relationship with Reece spoken of in such derogatory terms. But she didn't argue with Tad—she couldn't. Hadn't she thought the same thing more than once?

To his credit, Tad quickly realized that he'd overstepped his bounds, and rubbed her awkwardly on the back—as if a few pats could make up for what he'd said. "Look, Sarah, I'm sorry. That totally came out wrong. Its just that I'm not convinced this guy is good for you. And I'm sick and tired of watching you get screwed over."

"You act like it keeps happening. It's happened *once.* Yes, Mike was a loser. But Reece isn't like that. He calls every day to talk, has tried to make it home twice, but things keep cropping up. He'll be home when he can."

"Are you sure about that?"

"Yes." No—not by a long shot, but she couldn't tell her brother that. He was already down on Reece. That would be exacerbated if Tad found out Reece had left after making love to her. Tad would go through the roof. Or say, *I told you so.*

And right now, she couldn't handle either scenario. Not that she could blame him. Was she being blind?

Was it stupid to trust Reece with his dubious track record? Should she be more suspicious of the man who had already bailed on her twice?

But things had been different after he'd returned from California—he'd been so tender. So involved with Rose and the boys—and her. Shouldn't she be willing to trust him, just a little? Especially when she'd already given him her heart?

Maybe she should confront him when he got back from Hawaii. Tell him she wanted to know where they stood. Explain that she couldn't live in limbo forever—that it wasn't fair to the kids and it wasn't fair to her.

She was still brooding about the problem the next day, as she and Rose completed the grocery shopping for the week. Sarah had talked to Reece the night before—he'd called right before the kids' bedtime, like he always did—and he had seemed warm, loving. Completely focused on her and their unconventional family. But he'd also told her he wasn't going to make it back on Thursday as he'd thought. That the earliest he would make it home would be Monday or Tuesday of the following week.

She'd been as disappointed as the kids, but heartened by the disgust in his own tone. He'd sounded as upset as she was that it was going to be another six or seven days before he made it back.

And he *was* talking about making it back, had referred to her place as home numerous times in the conversations they'd had these past couple of weeks. Surely that counted for something?

Rose whined from her seat at the front of the basket, drawing Sarah's attention away from her internal debate. "I know, pumpkin," she murmured, pressing a kiss to the soft curls that had started growing on her baby's head. "You've been such a good girl, and we're almost done."

She turned the corner of the baby food aisle. "We've got to pick up a few things for you." Rose laughed and cooed as Sarah loaded the cart up with some of her favorite foods. "We want sweet potatoes and carrots and pears and apple blueberries. Yum, yum."

Rose blew a raspberry and Sarah laughed, delighted with her daughter. It was hard to imagine that a month ago, the little girl had been at death's door, and Sarah gave thanks every day that things had worked out the way they had.

She turned the next corner. "Okay, Rosie-posie. One last stop. We need diapers and wipes for you then we'll be out of here." But as she was putting a box of diapers into the cart, her gaze landed on the display across the aisle.

Her period was due and she didn't think she had enough tampons at home to last the month—better to stock up now than to make an unexpected run to the drugstore later. Especially with three kids and a limited amount of time. But as her hand closed over the box, something clicked in her head.

Her last period had been over a month before—she remembered because she'd had to stop at the drugstore on the way to open house at the boys' school. But that would mean—she counted in her head—that her period was nearly three weeks late.

Okay. Don't panic. She'd been under a lot of stress lately. That would throw anyone off.

Besides, Reece had always used protection. And none had broken, so surely she was safe.

Yet even as she started to put the tampons in her basket, she paused. Recounted to see if she'd somehow made a mistake. Freaking out when she realized her numbers were right on. She *was* over three weeks late—and her cycle was like clockwork. In fact, she'd only been late twice before in her entire life—and she'd been pregnant both of those times.

Panic was a cold fist within her as she cruised farther down the aisle to the pregnancy tests. It had only been eighteen months since she'd last had to buy one and she couldn't believe—absolutely could not believe—that she was standing here looking at them again.

Nauseous and cold to the bone, she picked up the most familiar brand and tossed it in her basket. Then all but ran for the checkout.

This couldn't be happening, she repeated over and over again in her head. She'd just started her first sexual relationship in six years. She absolutely could not be pregnant. Fate couldn't be that cruel. She'd already gone through two pregnancies and had had three children without a husband around. Could it be possible that she was gearing up for a fourth? The thought made her sick.

Taking one deep breath after another, trying desperately to focus on something besides the disaster looming, she packed her groceries into her car and then drove home as fast as she could—breaking a number of speeding laws in the process.

Once home, she didn't even bother to unload the groceries. Simply grabbed Rose and the pregnancy test and made a beeline for the house. With only a very quick stop to deposit an unhappy Rose in her playpen, she ran to the bathroom, tore open the test and took it before she could talk herself out of it.

Be negative, she whispered as she stared at the little results window. *Be negative, be negative.* The directions said to wait three minutes before checking, but in her experience if she was pregnant, the second line showed up right away.

And there it was—a second line next to the control line. She was pregnant.

Her legs went out from under her and she hit the ground, hard, but she was in so much shock she hardly registered the jolt. Pregnant. She was thirty-three. Pregnant. Unmarried. And alone—again.

Although, if she was completely honest, she'd been married to Mike when she'd gotten pregnant with the boys—just not when she delivered them. And with Rose, marriage hadn't been important. But with this one—her hand crept over her abdomen—with this one, it would have been nice to be married to a guy she knew was going to stick around for a while. She had absolutely no desire to go through a third pregnancy on her own.

She lifted the wand to look at it again, praying that

she had somehow misread the test. But she hadn't—both lines were still there in perfect clarity.

Sarah had no idea how long she sat there staring blankly at the pregnancy test, but eventually she talked herself into getting up and checking on Rose. The baby was playing contentedly with the odd assortment of toys at the bottom of her playpen, so Sarah went to unload the groceries.

As she carried a heavy box of water, Sarah couldn't help wondering how long she would be able to carry heavy stuff. How long before her energy started flagging—like it always did in the first trimester—and she had no chance of keeping up with the kids.

She glanced down at her feet, encased in a cute pair of sandals. How long before they swelled beyond recognition? Tears came to her eyes, but she quickly batted them away. If she started crying now, she might never stop. And she had too much to get done today to spend the day in hysterics, no matter how tempting the idea sounded.

With a sigh, she retrieved Rose. Then set the baby on the kitchen floor to watch as she unpacked the groceries and made lunch for both of them.

As she poured herself a big glass of milk, Sarah groaned. She hated milk with a passion and the idea of drinking it for the next nine months was almost enough to make her sick.

But she would adjust, she thought, as she glanced at the daughter she loved more than her own life. Didn't she always?

REECE HAD NEVER BEEN so happy to be home in his life. He'd been so anxious to see Sarah and the kids that he'd taken the red-eye in from Honolulu after his last meeting, which had gotten him home at ten in the morning instead of the much later evening flight he'd originally been booked into.

He hadn't called ahead, hadn't told Sarah to expect him, because he'd wanted to surprise her. But now that he stood in the middle of a silent house, he was the surprised one. Sarah was nowhere around—and neither was Rose.

He knew the boys were at school, but couldn't help wondering where his two best girls were. He'd hoped, naively it turned out, to have some time to spend with Sarah while Rose napped and before the boys got home.

It wasn't like her to be gone on a Tuesday, though. This was one of her work days, and according to the conversation they'd had the night before, her Web design business had suddenly gotten swamped. Which meant great things financially for her, but also difficulty in getting her schedule to match up. Maybe today was one of those days when the schedule didn't work.

Slowly, he carried his backpack and suitcase upstairs, cursing the entire Hawaii project to hell and back. He'd been gone almost a month and had hated every second of it. The trip should only have taken a week—two weeks at the most, but it had been a total disaster from beginning to end.

The worst part was, it hadn't even been his or Matt's

fault. The civil engineering company their client had hired to oversee the project had blown everything. It had taken him over a week to get his clients to understand that, then three more weeks to fix the damage the company had done in the meantime.

He was home now. That was what he needed to concentrate on. As he walked toward his bedroom, he could smell Sarah's perfume in the air. He'd only missed her by a few minutes. He cursed the traffic that had held him up.

He wanted to see her now, needed to hold her in his arms and reassure himself that everything was okay. She'd been different the past few days on the phone—stilted, abrupt. Almost as if she couldn't get him off the phone fast enough.

He'd tried to find out what was wrong, but she hadn't wanted to talk. She'd laughed and brushed him off, but he'd felt the vibes as clearly as if he was in the same room. Was Sarah getting cold feet? Was she freaking out over the Vanessa thing?

He couldn't blame her. He had his fair share of concerns. Had asked himself more than once what he was doing. But the fact of the matter was he cared about Sarah, a lot. He wanted to be with her and be with their children—he was already thinking of Justin and Johnny as his. Once he'd admitted that, he'd realized that everything else could take care of itself.

It would have to, because he wasn't giving up Sarah.

As he was getting out of the shower a few minutes later, he heard the garage door open. Excitement thrummed through him, and he threw on a pair of jeans before hitting the hallway at a run.

Sarah was already halfway up the stairs. "Reece?"

"I'm right here, love." Taking the remaining stairs two at a time, he swept her into his arms and kissed her full on the mouth.

Heat exploded between them immediately and before he knew it, he had his hand inside her blouse and was stroking her nipple. She felt so good, so warm and soft and good, that he wanted to bury himself in her forever.

"Where's Rose?" he asked as he skimmed his mouth across her jaw and began nibbling on her earlobe, gold hoop earring and all.

"Downstairs," she gasped, as she pulled away reluctantly. "I popped her on the floor, but she'll be scooting across the floor toward us at any second."

He was flabbergasted. "She's scooting now?"

"Yes." Sarah's smile was proud. "She's almost ready to start crawling, too. She's pushing up onto all fours, and even manages to move forward a little. But then she forgets what she's doing and collapses onto her tummy."

A wave of sorrow hit him so quickly that he didn't have a chance to hide it from Sarah.

"Hey, what's wrong?" she asked, running a hand over his suddenly grim mouth.

"I've missed so much—more than half her life, between what happened in the beginning and these last two trips."

"Hey, don't worry about it. She's down there now, and I bet she'd love to see her daddy."

Sarah's voice was light, but he sensed her withdrawal keenly. And her face wasn't right—her blue eyes were shadowed again and it looked like she'd lost weight.

"Hey." He grabbed her hand as she headed downstairs, stalling her progress. "Is everything okay? You look worn-out."

"Everything's great. I've just been busy. I picked up some new clients, plus I've been volunteering at the boys' school."

"You need to get more rest. I'm sorry I had to leave."

"I wish you'd stop saying that." She headed down the stairs, tugging him along behind her. "Believe me, I know all about having to make a living."

"I know, but—" He broke off when he got his first glimpse of his daughter. "She's grown so much!" he exclaimed, heading toward her.

"She has. Almost two full inches."

"And she's got hair."

"Aren't the curls great?"

"They're beautiful—just like her mother's." Holding his arms out to pick her up, he said, "Hey, Rosie-posie," in the singsong voice he knew she loved. But instead of coming to him, she started to cry as she scooted across the floor toward Sarah.

"What's wrong?" he asked, bewildered. "Doesn't she remember me?"

He'd said the last as a joke, but judging from the looks on Rosie's and Sarah's face, he was suddenly afraid he had hit on exactly what the problem was.

"I was gone too long." He walked forward slowly, his

arms actually aching with the need to hold his daughter. "She really doesn't remember me."

"She will," Sarah answered soothingly, keeping her voice pitched low as she rubbed her baby's back. "Give her a minute."

He gave her several, and Rose finally loosened up enough to let him hold her. It was obvious she recognized his voice, but still wasn't sure how to respond to him. Even their favorite games only got a smile out of her—the giggles of a month before were long gone.

By the time Sarah suggested he try and put Rose down for a nap, he was emotionally exhausted. Bowing out with a claim of jet lag, he went up to his room and spent the next hour staring at the ceiling.

His fantasy homecoming had ended up as just that— a fantasy. And the reality of it was turning out to be one hell of a nightmare. His daughter didn't remember him and his lover seemed less than enthusiastic at his presence. He could still remember the slight frown on her face as she climbed the stairs, almost as if she was disappointed to see him in her house.

What a joke he was. A failure. He'd totally screwed up the best things in his life—with his unnecessary trip to San Francisco followed closely by this one to Hawaii. How could he have expected things to stay the same? A month was a long time in baby time—seven weeks even longer. And that's how long he'd been gone over the past three months—*seven weeks*. His only at-home time had been when the baby was sick and the weeks immediately following her release from the hospital.

Was it any wonder things weren't going as he'd planned? He was a bigger idiot than he'd thought.

A loser.

A failure.

The words hit him hard, made him shudder— shadows of the names his father used to call his brother. Memories of what Vanessa would shout at him when she lost her temper, knowing how he felt about the subject. At the time he'd been able to let the insults roll of his back, secure in himself and his place in the world.

But since he'd moved in with Sarah those words had been haunting him. It seemed no matter what he did here, he couldn't get it right.

A knock on the door startled him out of his self-imposed misery. "Can I come in?" Sarah opened the door slowly, almost as if she was afraid of rejection.

"Sure." He scooted over, then patted the spot next to him on the bed. When she eyed it nervously, her teeth worrying her lower lip, he felt worse than ever. What did it say about him that his lover wouldn't even sit on a bed with him?

"Sarah?"

She seemed to have gotten over whatever it was that had upset her. Climbing onto the bed, she lay down next to him and put her head on his shoulder.

They lay like that for a while. Quiet. Content. Drifting along until their hearts and breathing were as one. This was what he'd been missing, Reece reflected, even more than the sex. He'd missed the feel of her against him, her softness so different than the hardness of his own body. The spicy, cinnamon smell of her that wrapped itself around him. The sweet sound of her breathing, the soft thud of her heartbeat.

He'd missed it all, and feared that if this didn't work out—if he failed here as he had failed Vanessa—he would feel that absence the rest of his life.

"So tell me about Hawaii." Sarah's voice was low, inviting and it skated along his nerve endings, stoking the fire that had been burning inside him for days.

"It was a disaster." Rolling onto his side, he pulled her more firmly against him, until her breasts pressed against his chest, her nipples hard pebbles he longed to taste. "Completely screwed up."

"How?"

Was her voice more breathless than it had been a minute ago, he wondered as he fought the sexual haze that had him in its grip.

"They cut corners by hiring this CE firm—"

"CE?"

"Civil Engineering. Anyway, the firm underbid its competitors by a significant amount, but for whatever reason, that didn't raise any red flags in the client. Until they started failing inspections and the building went to hell fast."

He ran his lips along the fragile line of her jaw, relishing the fresh mango taste and smell of her face cream. "You always smell so delicious," he murmured. "I spent hours fantasizing about your scent while I was gone."

"Hours?" She leaned back enough to look him in the eye. "Really?"

He took a deep breath, taking her all the way into his lungs and holding her there for long seconds. "Absolutely. You smell fantastic." He buried his face in her neck and began to nibble his way along the slender, elegant column.

She giggled, a very un-Sarahlike sound, but one that revved his engine a little higher. "Sarah, forgive me, but I need to be inside you. I know you want to talk." He gasped as her hands skimmed over his stomach, toying with the button of his jeans. "And I swear, we'll talk later. But now—"

"I thought you'd never ask."

Her mouth closed over his, her tongue running along his bottom lip until he nearly forgot to breathe. It was a long time before either one of them even thought about speaking.

CHAPTER SEVENTEEN

"HEY, REECE, could you come here for a second?"
Sarah called.

"What's wrong?" he asked, coming down the stairs.

"How do you know something's wrong?"

"That little strain you get in your voice. It usually
means the boys did something." With a grin, he pulled
her into his arms and planted one on her. And while he'd
meant it to be a quick, hello kind of kiss, her lips parted
and he found himself lingering. His tongue swept into
her mouth to tangle with hers and she tasted so good he
didn't want to let her go.

He'd never before understood why anyone would
want to freeze time. For him, there were always other
things to do—mountains to climb, people to meet, buildings to create. But this week he'd found himself looking
around and thinking that everything was perfect—that
there was absolutely nothing in his life that he would
change. Rose was happy and healthy and growing, as
were the boys. And Sarah. Sarah was unbelievable.
Warm and exciting and willing and understanding—
everything he could ever want in a woman and more.

Yes, he thought, as he reluctantly lifted his mouth

from hers, if he had the ability to freeze time, these were the moments he would choose to keep. For the first time in a year, he was happy. For the first time in a year, he was whole. That was the magic of Sarah.

And if she had a shadow in her eyes sometimes when she watched him, then so be it. They came to each other with pasts darker than most people had. It would be selfish for him to expect her to be perfectly content all the time.

"So, what did you want?" he asked again, his hands creeping around to cup her bottom. Lifting her onto her tippy-toes, he pressed himself against her and was rewarded when her eyes glazed over.

She sighed, then leaned against his chest as her hips moved restlessly against his. "The boys clogged the toilet again."

He couldn't keep the amusement from his voice when he asked, "What was it this time?"

"A train." She shook her head, but her lips were curved reluctantly. "They wanted to see if it could survive the 'whirling vortex of terror.'"

He laughed—he couldn't help himself. "Where do they come up with this stuff?"

She nodded to her sons, who were currently sitting in front of the TV. "Saturday morning cartoons."

"Ah, yes. Of course."

"So, do me a favor and see if you can fix it. Otherwise I need to get Vince out here."

"My masculine instincts are enraged." He patted her on the bottom before heading toward the bathroom.

"How dare you doubt me? Haven't I proven, numerous times, that I can face down the whirling vortex of terror and live to tell the tale?"

She laughed, as he'd intended—a full belly laugh that did nothing to calm his arousal. "I'm so sorry. I certainly didn't mean to cast aspersions on your manliness."

He gave her a mock scowl. "You don't look anywhere near repentant enough when you say that."

"Does that mean you're going to have to punish me?" Her eyes sparkled with sassiness.

"I'm afraid so." He nodded gravely, barely keeping a big-ass grin from escaping. "You've cast aspersions on me and my abilities and that can not be allowed. I will be back for you—after I've conquered the vortex—and you will be made to pay."

"Ooh, I can't wait." Sarah winked at him, giving her hips an extra wiggle as she strolled toward the kitchen. "Oh, and hey, mighty warrior." She tossed the words over her shoulder.

"Yes?" He drew his gaze away from her pert, rounded bottom with difficulty.

"The plunger's next to the vortex. Go to town."

This time he couldn't stop the laugh from escaping. No, things weren't perfect with Sarah—they were both too hotheaded and opinionated for peace to reign very long—but life was never dull. And he was finding out how much he enjoyed the added spice—and Sarah's proclivity for getting in the last word.

It only took him a couple of minutes to clear the

toilet—the boys had used one of their smallest trains this time, thank God. Shaking his head, he went into the kitchen to show Sarah what he'd recovered.

Rolling her eyes, she said, "I don't know what to do with them. They promised they'd stop doing this."

He laughed. "Actually, if I remember correctly, all they promised was to stop flushing the action figures. They didn't say anything about other toys."

"My mistake," Sarah said with a smile. "Who would have thought?"

Reece studied her for a second. Though her smile seemed real enough, it didn't quite reach her eyes. Crossing the room, he pulled her against him and started rubbing her shoulders. "You've been hunched over that computer too long. Your muscles are like rock."

This time her laugh was not amused. "I don't think it's the computer work doing that."

"No?" He dug in his fingers a little deeper to get out the knots. "Then what is?"

She turned to look at him and her mouth was set in a grim line. Her eyes were shadowed and she looked almost frightened.

"What's wrong, Sarah?"

She took a deep breath, and looked like she wanted to be anywhere but here. To give her credit, however, she kept her feet planted and her eyes on his when she said, "I'm pregnant, Reece."

At first, he thought he'd misunderstood her, but her small, self-deprecating smile spoke for itself.

Cold chills shot down his spine as he struggled to sort

out his emotions. How had this happened? He'd been careful, had used protection. She *couldn't* be pregnant.

Except Sarah would never say something that wasn't true. She was honest to a fault, so completely forthright that sometimes it shocked him.

He didn't know what to say, was so shell-shocked that he could barely string two thoughts together. But she was looking at him expectantly, so he finally managed to ask, "Are you okay?"

The look she gave him was incredulous—and annoyed. "I'm fine. It's not like I haven't done this before."

"I know. It's just—" He stared at her still-flat stomach. His baby was inside her. *His* baby. And this time, it had gotten there the old-fashioned way—no doctors or clinics involved.

He still couldn't wrap his mind around it.

"Well, say something."

"I don't know what to say." He pulled his gaze from Sarah's midsection with difficulty. A thousand thoughts and feelings were bombarding him at once and he wasn't sure which to act on. Shock, fear, concern warred within him, mixing with the beginnings of a happiness that was wholly unexpected.

Finally, when the silence between them had dragged on for too long, he asked, "When?"

She raised an eyebrow, her eyes cool despite the brief flare of panic he'd seen there. "When did I get pregnant?"

"When did you find out?" He'd already figured out when it had happened—the only logical time would have been in the weeks leading up to his trip to Hawaii.

"A little over a week ago.

"A week ago?" That put a small dent in the shock. "You didn't tell me."

"You weren't here."

He winced at the harshness in her voice. "I'm sorry about that. Sorry you had to find out alone."

She shrugged. "I'm used to being alone."

For the first time, anger pierced through the other emotions. Not at the pregnancy, but at Sarah's attitude. "Well, you're not alone now."

She didn't answer, but her expression spoke louder than any words. *For how long,* she asked silently. *How long will you stick around this time?* And though he knew he'd given her reason to doubt him in the past, he couldn't help being hurt. Anymore than he could help the anger that continued to grow. He'd thought they were past this, thought she was learning to trust him.

"So why tell me now?" He forced himself to remain calm. "I've been home five days."

"I was trying to figure out the right time to tell you."

He glanced at the train he'd fished out of the toilet. "And this was it?"

"I don't know. It seemed like I needed to tell you before you made any more plans. For us," she clarified at his confused look.

"And your pregnancy would stop me from making plans?"

"I don't know," she repeated again.

He gritted his teeth. "Well, what exactly do you know?"

"Reece." Her chin tilted and the defiance was back,

almost as if she blamed him for overreacting. But hell, what else could he do? With each word she spoke it became more apparent that she didn't trust him. That she hadn't told him because she didn't think he'd stick by her.

"I needed time to sort out what I was going to do."

His blood ran cold. "What does that mean?"

"I need to make plans, figure out how I'm going to balance a fourth child when I can barely handle three."

"Don't you mean *we?* How are *we* going to balance a fourth child?" He studied her, felt his anger grow until it dwarfed everything else.

"Yes. No." She looked absolutely miserable. "I don't know what I mean."

"Well, that's interesting. You act like I don't even get a vote here."

"That's not what I said. You're being deliberately mean about this and I don't understand why."

"It's not that hard to figure out. You're carrying my baby and didn't see fit to tell me."

"I did tell you."

"Now. After more than a week's gone by. After you figured out what *you* wanted to do."

"You make it sound like that's a bad thing."

"It is a bad thing! We're in this together, Sarah. You should have come to me, should have trusted me about this as soon as you found out. So that we could figure out what to do together."

She worried her lower lip between her teeth before finally blurting, "I don't have the best luck with men and pregnancy, Reece. I was scared, wanted some time to come to terms with being pregnant and alone—again—before I told anyone."

"I'm not *anyone*. I'm the father of the baby you're carrying." He paused, let her other words sink in. "And you're not alone."

"I'm not?"

At first he bristled at the sarcastic question, then registered—with shock—that Sarah was being sincere, not sarcastic. She really thought he was going to leave her to go through this on her own.

The realization cut like a knife and he found himself lashing out at her. "Is that what you think of me? That I'd get you pregnant and then abandon you?"

She didn't answer. But then she didn't have to. Her arched brow said it all—that and the memories that swarmed between them of another pregnancy, another baby.

"That was different, damn it," he said.

"Was it?" she asked. "All I know is that I've been pregnant twice and both times the men have run as far and as fast from the responsibility as they could get. Forgive me if it took me a while to work up to dealing with it for a third time."

"You don't trust me." He felt his knees tremble as they got to the crux of the matter. "You don't think I'll be here for you."

"It's not that—"

"Don't prevaricate—it doesn't become you. It's exactly that and we both know it. *You don't trust me.*"

"How can I? It's not like you've been exactly reliable so far, right? Ignoring me after Vanessa died, ignoring Rose. Running off to San Francisco at the first sign of something bigger than what you wanted."

The words hit with the precision of laser-guided missiles. He'd failed her—every step of the way and now she was punishing him for it. "You told me you understood."

"I do. But that didn't make it any easier to handle." She reached out to him, but he shrugged off her hand. He was angry—furious—and afraid her touch would only stoke the furnace of his rage.

"Can you see this from my point of view?" she asked.

"I am. And I understand that I screwed up with you, royally—and more than once. But I thought you understood. Thought you knew that I would never do that to you again."

She wrapped her arms around herself and looked away. And nearly broke his heart. After everything he'd done to prove himself to her, she still didn't get it. Couldn't get it. He'd messed up and he had been a fool to think that he could make things better. It was completely ridiculous to think that they could just move on from his many and myriad failures.

"Look, I'm sorry. Sorrier than I can say that I put you through that. But Sarah, don't these past weeks count for anything? Anything at all?"

"Of course they do, Reece. I was going to tell you."

"Right. But you had to work up the nerve to do so. Am I that scary? My reactions that unpredictable?"

"No! It's just…" Her voice trailed off.

"It's exactly that." Turning, he jogged up the stairs without another word.

"Where are you going?" she demanded.

He grabbed his wallet, quickly slid on his favorite pair of running shoes and was back down in less than a minute. "Out."

The word seemed to send her reeling back and for a moment he felt guilty. But he couldn't stay in this house with her for another second, couldn't deal with this argument right now. Not when the pain was seething inside of him, along with a need to lash out at her that he refused to give in to. Better that he calm down and they discuss this later, when they could both be rational, than he take the chance of saying something he might regret now.

"So you're leaving? Just like that?" Her voice was furious, her face devoid of emotion. "You find out I'm pregnant and you can't get out the door fast enough?"

Fury seethed, consumed him. "Is that what you think?"

"It's what I know. And you ask why I didn't tell you right away?" She swept her arm toward the front door. "Don't let it hit you on your way out, Reece. We don't need you—we never have and we never will."

Gritting his teeth, forcing back the hurt that was wildly alive within him, he headed for the door at a dead run. And didn't look back.

SARAH STOOD STARING at the door for long minutes after Reece left and still she couldn't believe it. He'd walked out—no, *run* out—without so much as a backward glance. Even as she'd told herself this would happen, there was a part of her that had been sure he'd stay. Had wanted him to stay.

Even after she'd heard his truck start up and the tires squeal as he headed away from the house much too quickly, she stayed where she was. Waiting for him to understand. Waiting for him to come back.

But he didn't, and eventually the kids needed lunch and naps and mommy time. So she went through the motions of the day, all the time her mind and heart focused solely on Reece.

Had he really run away from her—from the baby they'd made together? Had he really turned his back on all of them? Again?

Her thoughts were such a muddle, their conversation such a blur of hurt and fear and anger that she wasn't sure exactly what had happened. The only thing she knew for certain was that she was pregnant. And Reece was gone.

But for how long?

Was this it, then? Had he decided she was too much trouble, with her three—soon to be four—kids and her house that kept breaking and her past that sometimes got the best of her?

She had a hard time accepting that. He'd been attentive, loving, one hundred percent there for her and the kids. And all her fears had seemed groundless—or at least, minimized.

She'd been working up to telling him about the baby, going over options, deciding what was the best way to break the news to him. But she had been scared. No matter how wonderful Reece had been, he was still the man who had abandoned her when she'd needed him most. Combined with her old fears and insecurities, that was a hard thing to move past.

But she'd been trying—trying to trust him, trying to trust her own judgment more. Hadn't she waited—albeit nervously—for him to get back from Hawaii? The old Sarah might have written him off right away, but she'd held on. Sure, she'd had doubts, but she'd trusted him. Didn't that count for anything?

Apparently not.

She glanced at the clock and realized Reece had been gone nearly six hours. Where was he? Why was he doing this to her when he knew she had abandonment issues?

By eleven o'clock that night, after the children were in bed and the house was quiet, anger had given way to worry. Where was he? Why wasn't he home yet? What if he was hurt somewhere and she didn't know? What if he wasn't?

And the most overwhelming question of all. Was he coming home at all?

Maybe that was it. Maybe he wasn't coming back.

She'd put all her faith in him, put as much trust as she had in him, and she'd been wrong. Again. He wasn't any different than her father and Mike, merely less honest about it.

CHAPTER EIGHTEEN

REECE STARED at the pile of leaves he'd raked in complete and total dissatisfaction. Oh, there was nothing wrong with the pile—except for the fact that the lawn service that he'd hired to take care of his house hadn't been doing their job. But it was what the pile represented that had him so annoyed. The fact that, like these leaves, he was unwanted and out of place. Obviously he didn't fit in at Sarah's—not like he'd thought he had. But he didn't fit here, at his house, either.

When he'd left Sarah's yesterday, he'd intended to get some air before returning to confront her. He'd needed to let his temper simmer for a while. then calm before he said something he couldn't take back.

But when, after hours of driving around, he was no calmer than when he'd started, he'd ended up here. At his home. He winced at the description, because he'd known it wasn't home before he'd been in the house five minutes. His home was fifteen minutes away, in Sarah's too-crowded, too-messy, too-noisy house. And he missed it, more than he'd thought possible.

But he'd stuck it out here. Had spent the night, even though he'd longed for the warmth of Sarah's body next to his in bed. Had gone down the street for breakfast, as his house no longer had any food in it. And had brooded the entire time.

Coming back here was a double whammy, he decided as he shuffled the leaves into bags. Not only did he not feel at home here, but even worse, he could no longer feel Vanessa here. Last night, he'd sat on the couch, mindlessly watching a ball game when he'd realized his feelings for Vanessa were no longer an ache that couldn't be filled.

Oh, he missed her smile, missed the way she could be in tune with him. But he didn't miss her the way one missed a lover—or a wife. As if his hand had been chopped off or his heart removed. No, that pain was gone when he thought of Vanessa—but very much in evidence when he thought about how badly he'd blown it with Sarah.

Why had he freaked out like that—yelling at her, telling her she didn't trust him? Why should she trust him when he didn't even trust himself? When he continued to give her reason after reason not to trust him?

He liked to pretend that those months after Van's death hadn't happened—liked to imagine how different his life would have been if he'd stepped up and helped Sarah when he should have. But he didn't know what his life would be like right now if he'd done his duty all those months ago. Would he still be with Sarah, loving her? Or would he have been so blinded by guilt at the thought of touching Vanessa's best friend that he would have let the best thing in his life pass him by?

He still had twinges of guilt, regrets that Vanessa had

died while he got to live. But he refused to feel bad about loving Sarah. She'd brought color and sunshine back into a life that had gone abysmally gray. He would love her for that alone.

Shaking his head, he went into the house and drank a tall glass of water, hoping it would quench the thirst for Sarah that was a physical ache inside of him. It didn't work, of course, only made him feel lonelier as he thought of sitting around Sarah's kitchen, drinking coffee and laughing at some antic of Justin's while they all ate the blueberry pancakes he had made.

He was the official breakfast maker in the house, as Sarah wasn't at her best early in the morning. But she handled the midnight shifts with the kids like a pro, whereas he was usually stumbling around by eleven o'clock, exhausted.

Funny how he'd never noticed how much they complemented each other. How one's strengths played into the other's weaknesses. Just one more way his relationship with Sarah was so different than the one he'd had with Vanessa.

Stopping suddenly on his way out of the house, Reece let his thoughts play back in his mind. There was something significant there—he could feel it. He just needed to figure out what it was. Sarah was different than he was, always changing. Never the same. Her moods were quicksilver—she could be furious one minute then laughing the next, whatever had made her angry forgotten. Or if not forgotten, at least buried deep. That's when it hit him—Sarah had as many vulnerabilities and worries as Vanessa had had. She was better at hiding them, so that she always appeared strong, calm, in control. Yet she wasn't. Inside she was as big a mess as he was. But whereas he was afraid of failing—himself and others—she was afraid of trusting anyone but herself.

Why? Because everyone, including him, had let her down. Over and over and over again. Was it any wonder she had trouble trusting him? Any wonder she hadn't rushed to tell him about the baby? Hell, when he thought of how he'd reacted to the news—with anger and accusations instead of happiness and concern for her—he was pissed enough to kick his own ass.

Why was it so easy to live up to everyone else's expectations—no matter how high—yet so difficult to do anything but live down to Sarah's? He was an idiot.

Yesterday, Sarah had needed reassurances and understanding. Instead, he'd been awful to her. Had yelled at her then did the one thing she'd expected him to do all along—he'd left. He might have known he walked out until he could calm himself down, but did he bother to tell Sarah that? No, he'd left her standing stricken, and wondering whether he was ever coming back.

Racing into the house, he grabbed the keys to his truck. Then he was flying across the lawn in an effort to get to Sarah. As he hopped in the truck and took off, he glanced in the rearview mirror at the house he'd shared with Vanessa for the better half of a decade. It was time to sell it, he thought. Time to move on. Time to close the escape hatch, so that Sarah understood she was stuck with him—whether she wanted him or not.

Because this time, he wasn't going anywhere. And neither was she.

SARAH WAS UPSTAIRS playing with the boys and trying to muster some enthusiasm for the rest of her life when she heard the front door slam. With her heart in her throat, she handed the red train she'd been driving to her oldest son and went to confront Reece.

She'd done a lot of thinking while he'd been gone—and she'd reached some conclusions. She had been wrong not to tell him about the baby, not to trust him with that information. He was nothing like her father and Mike, and she should have known it. After all, the reason he'd abandoned her after Vanessa's death was because he'd had such a hard time letting go of his wife.

When Reece loved, he did it unconditionally and absolutely and Sarah had been ridiculously stupid to let her old fears stand in the way of her understanding something so fundamentally important.

But he'd been wrong, too. He'd had no business running away—not to San Francisco after he'd kissed her and not yesterday when he'd left to lick his wounds. And that's what he'd been doing. As she'd lain in bed staring at the ceiling last night, she'd come to some kind of understanding of him. And that understanding had brought her a peace that had been lacking in her life for far too long.

When Reece left, it wasn't because he wasn't going

to come back. It was because, like a wounded animal, he needed to lick his wounds in private. He needed to brood and get his mind around whatever it was that had bothered him. When that was finished, he would come back, ready for whatever else life threw at him.

That didn't give him the right to take off and stay out all night and scare her to death. And she had an entire speech prepared to help her get that message across.

Except as soon as she saw him taking the stairs two at a time, every thought she'd managed to string together in the past twenty-four hours flew out of her head. And all she could think about was how good he looked and how much she wanted him and how happy she wanted to make him.

"Sarah!" he called as he clamored up the steps to her. "Sarah, I was an ass. A total and complete idiot."

"What?" Everything inside of her froze and for a second she was sure she'd misheard him.

When he got to the landing at the top of the stairs, he grabbed her hands. His were ice-cold, but his face was alive with passion and excitement. "This morning, I realized there was a lot I forgot to say yesterday. I let myself get so blinded by my hurt and anger that I couldn't see how you were feeling. I didn't tell you what else I felt, didn't realize how much you needed to hear it."

"What are you talking about?" For a moment hope was bright and painful within her.

"I want you and I want our baby. I'm thrilled that you're pregnant and that I get to be here, every step of the way, for this baby. And I'm not going anywhere. If you want me out of your life, you'll have to drag me kicking and screaming away from you and Rose and the boys." His eyes dropped to her waist. "And this baby. I want all five of you, more than I ever thought it possible to want anything."

"Reece—" There were tears in her eyes, a lump in her throat so big she could barely get the words out. "Don't say it if you don't mean it. I couldn't stand—"

"Oh, I mean it, Sarah. I've spent my life avoiding messing up, yet all I've done is mess up with you."

"I understand." She reached for him and he pulled her into his arms, ran his lips over her hair and down to her mouth for one brief moment before moving away slightly.

"No, you don't. Because I've never told you. When Vanessa died, I was lost. Completely broken. Not just because I had lost my wife, which was horrible enough, but because I'd failed her. Failed to be a good enough husband, failed to be strong enough father material, failed to keep her alive."

"That's ridiculous. Vanessa loved you."

"Yes, and I loved her. But things hadn't been good between us for a long time. She'd been so obsessed with having a baby that it had taken over every part of her life, and the fact that I couldn't give her one was a constant failure on my part."

"But it wasn't your fault Vanessa couldn't conceive."

"Intellectually, I knew that. But as I watched my wife slowly losing her mind, I felt like I should be able to do something. She cried herself to sleep every single night and I couldn't make her feel better. She went through torturous surgeries and procedures and I couldn't take her pain away.

"Do you know how that makes a man feel?" he asked, as he closed his eyes against the memories. "Like's he's useless. Worthless. Like he's failed the most important person in his life. And when she died—" He choked up and Sarah's heart broke for him. "When she died, it shattered me, because keeping her safe was one more thing I'd failed to do."

"Reece—"

"No." He shook his head. "Let me finish. I know I should have been there for you, Sarah, but I couldn't be. I was no good for myself, no good for anyone for months after the funeral. Self-destructive, angry, I couldn't help myself let alone you or Rose."

"It's okay."

"No, it's not. You went through hell because I was too weak to get myself together. And I'm sorrier about that than I can ever tell you." He paused, and brought his hands up to cup her face. "But I'm here now. And I'm not going anywhere ever again. You'll never have to worry about raising our children on your own."

Her heart melted. "I know, Reece. Last night I realized that not trusting you was stupid. You're the very best man I know and if I can't make it work with you, then there's no one in the world I could make it work with. I know there's no one else in the world I *want* to be with, no other man I want to help raise my children— all of them."

"I want to adopt the boys. I already consider them mine, but they need to know that I feel about them the same way I feel about Rose, the same way I'll feel about the new baby."

"I love you, Reece Sandler."

"I love you, Sarah Martin. And I want to marry you as soon as humanly possible."

"Marriage?" Sarah's stomach jumped at the word, and her heart pounded even faster.

"You still don't get it, do you?" he asked, a smile on his face. "I'm not letting you go—we're forever. You, me and the kids. I just hope that's long enough."

He pulled her into his arms, tucking her against his chest so that she could feel his heart pounding as riotously as her own. And that's when she truly began to believe.

Sarah shuddered with the realization that all her dreams were coming true—dreams she hadn't even known she'd had until he'd given them to her. A man who understood her and who loved her anyway. A man strong enough to stick around—for her and her children—through good times and bad.

They weren't fancy dreams, nor were they unusual ones. But they were hers and Reece had made them come true. He said she brought the sunshine into his life, but she knew the truth. For her and the boys and Rose—and this new baby—he was the sunshine.

And that was more than enough.

* * * * *

ALEXANDROS KAREDES, SNOW DUSTING the shoulders of his leather jacket and glittering like jewels in his dark hair, stood at the door. Maria felt the blood drain from her head.

"Good evening, Ms. Santos."

His voice was as she remembered it. Deep. Husky. Perfect English, but with the faintest hint of a Greek accent. And cold, as cold as it had been that awful morning she would never forget, when he'd accused her of horrible things, called her terrible names....

"Aren't you going to ask me in?"

She fought for composure. Last time they'd faced each other, they'd been on his turf. Now they were on hers. She was in command here, and that meant everything.

"There's a sign on the door downstairs," she said, her tone every bit as frigid as his. "It says, 'No soliciting or vagrants.'"

His lips drew back in a wolfish grin. "Very amusing."

"What do you want, Prince Alexandros?"

A tight smile eased across his mouth and it killed her

that even now, knowing he was a vicious, arrogant man, she couldn't help but notice what a handsome mouth it was. Chiseled. Generous. Beautiful, like the rest of him, which made him living proof that beauty could, indeed, be only skin deep.

"Such formality, Maria. You were hardly so proper the last time we were together."

She knew his choice of words was deliberate. She felt her face heat; she couldn't help that but she damned well didn't have to let him lure her into a verbal sparring match.

"I'll ask you once more, your highness. What do you want?"

"Ask me in and I'll tell you."

"I have no intention of asking you in. Tell me why you're here or don't. It's your choice, just as it will be my choice to shut the door in your face."

He laughed. It infuriated her but she could hardly blame him. He was tall—six two, six three—and though he stood with one shoulder leaning against the door frame, hands tucked casually into the pockets of the jacket, his pose was deceptive. He was strong, with the leanly muscled body of a well-trained athlete.

She remembered his body with painful clarity. The feel of him under her hands. The power of him moving over her. The taste of him on her tongue.

Suddenly, he straightened, his laughter gone. "I have not come this distance to stand in your doorway," he said coldly, "and I am not going to leave until I am ready to do so. I suggest you stand aside and stop behaving like a petulant child."

A petulant child? Was that what he thought? This man who had spent hours making love to her and had then accused her of—of trading her body for profit?

Except it had not been love, it had been sex. And the sooner she got rid of him, the better.

She let go of the doorknob and stepped aside. "You have five minutes."

He strolled past her, bringing cold air and the scent of the night with him. She swung toward him, arms folded. He reached past her, pushed the door closed, then folded his arms, too. She wanted to open the door again but she'd be damned if she was going to get into a who's-in-charge-here argument with him. She was in charge, and he would surely see a tussle over the ground rules as a sign of weakness.

Instead, she looked past him at the big clock above her work table.

"Ten seconds gone," she said briskly. "You're wasting time, your highness."

"What I have to say will take longer than five minutes."

"Then you'll just have to learn to economize. More than five minutes, I'll call the police."

Instantly, his hand was wrapped around her wrist. He tugged her toward him, his dark-chocolate eyes almost black with anger.

"You do that and I'll tell every tabloid shark I can

contact about how Maria Santos tried to buy a five-hundred-thousand-dollar commission by seducing a prince." He smiled thinly. "They'll lap it up."

* * * * *

What will it take for this billionaire prince
to realize he's falling in love with his mistress…?
Look for
BILLIONAIRE PRINCE, PREGNANT MISTRESS
by Sandra Marton
Available July 2009
from Harlequin Presents®.

We'll be spotlighting a different series every month
throughout 2009 to celebrate our 60th anniversary.

Look for Harlequin® Presents in July!

TWO CROWNS, TWO ISLANDS, ONE LEGACY
A royal family, torn apart by pride and its lust for
power, reunited by purity and passion

Step into the world of Karedes
beginning this July with

BILLIONAIRE PRINCE,
PREGNANT MISTRESS
by
Sandra Marton

Eight volumes to collect and treasure!

You're invited to join our Tell Harlequin Reader Panel!

By joining our new reader panel you will:

- Receive Harlequin® books—they are FREE and yours to keep with no obligation to purchase anything!
- Participate in fun online surveys
- Exchange opinions and ideas with women just like you
- Have a say in our new book ideas and help us publish the best in women's fiction

In addition, you will have a chance to win great prizes and receive special gifts! See Web site for details. Some conditions apply. Space is limited.

To join, visit us at
www.TellHarlequin.com.

REQUEST YOUR FREE BOOKS!

2 FREE NOVELS PLUS 2 FREE GIFTS!

HARLEQUIN®

Super Romance®

Exciting, emotional, unexpected!

YES! Please send me 2 FREE Harlequin® Superromance® novels and my 2 FREE gifts (gifts are worth about $10). After receiving them, if I don't wish to receive any more books, I can return the shipping statement marked "cancel." If I don't cancel, I will receive 6 brand-new novels every month and be billed just $4.69 per book in the U.S. or $5.24 per book in Canada. That's a savings of close to 15% off the cover price! It's quite a bargain! Shipping and handling is just 50¢ per book*. I understand that accepting the 2 free books and gifts places me under no obligation to buy anything. I can always return a shipment and cancel at any time. Even if I never buy another book from Harlequin, the two free books and gifts are mine to keep forever.

135 HDN EYLG   336 HDN EYLS

Name	(PLEASE PRINT)	
Address		Apt. #
City	State/Prov.	Zip/Postal Code

Signature (if under 18, a parent or guardian must sign)

Mail to the **Harlequin Reader Service:**
IN U.S.A.: P.O. Box 1867, Buffalo, NY 14240-1867
IN CANADA: P.O. Box 609, Fort Erie, Ontario L2A 5X3

Not valid to current subscribers of Harlequin Superromance books.

**Are you a current subscriber of Harlequin Superromance books
and want to receive the larger-print edition?
Call 1-800-873-8635 today!**

* Terms and prices subject to change without notice. Prices do not include applicable taxes. Sales tax applicable in N.Y. Canadian residents will be charged applicable provincial taxes and GST. Offer not valid in Quebec. This offer is limited to one order per household. All orders subject to approval. Credit or debit balances in a customer's account(s) may be offset by any other outstanding balance owed by or to the customer. Please allow 4 to 6 weeks for delivery. Offer available while quantities last.

Your Privacy: Harlequin is committed to protecting your privacy. Our Privacy Policy is available online at www.eHarlequin.com or upon request from the Reader Service. From time to time we make our lists of customers available to reputable third parties who may have a product or service of interest to you. If you would prefer we not share your name and address, please check here. ☐